Copyright © D.W. Jackson

Names, characters, and incidents are products of the author's imagination, or are used fictitiously. Any resemblance to actual event, organizations, or persons, is entirely coincidental and beyond the intent of the author.

All rights reserved. No part of this book may be reproduced or transmitted in any form or by any means whatsoever. Including photocopying, recording or by any information storage and retrieval system, without written permission from the author.

If you would like to be placed on a list to be notified of future works from this author or if you would like to comment on the book you may send a request to dwjacks01@yahoo.com

Your email address will not be sold or given to any third parties or used outside to promote other works.

Note From The Author

This book was edited and proofread by proofreadingservies.com on 2/9/14, with the exception on the copyright page and this one.

As you might be aware internet pricey is a very widespread. If you have not paid for this book and enjoyed it, think about paying for an official copy. I am not a big publisher and editing, cover costs, as well as other expenses come directly out of my pocket. I love to write and I can continue to do so by my readers, who I am grateful for. Instead of buying the book, if you wish, you can make a direct contribution to my paypal account at dwjacks01@yahoo.com. I understand that times are hard for a great deal of people but even one cent added up over time can help a great deal in keeping me writing. Thank you for reading and I hope you have a great year.

CHAPTER I

Trying to enjoy what little time he had to himself, Mark gazed at the clouds floating above him. Lately, his mind had been consumed with the upcoming sale, and his nerves had been on edge. His recent fourte-enth birthday meant he would soon find himself on the auction block, along with many of the others he had grown up with during his time at the academy. Like the others at the academy, his mother had saved enough to have him sent there to be trained, in hopes that he could be sold for a high price.

Mark remembered little of his family, other than the fact that he had lived on a fair-sized farm where, from the time he could barely walk, he was forced to work, doing whatever his small frame would allow. His mother had been upset that her firstborn was male and therefore was unable to be the heir she wanted. In hopes of turning a profit, she had spent two hundred gold pieces, to send him to the academy that was famous for turning out the most sought-after slaves in all of the queendom. After his sale, his mother would receive 80 percent of the profit, and though he didn't like the idea of making her coin, it seemed she would do quite well.

Mark had heard the academy mothers talking. They expected him to be their prize at the upcoming auction. Though he was not very tall, at only five foot eight, he had a very muscular build. Mixed with his short blond hair and his bright blue eyes, he was a hand-some and a somewhat imposing figure for someone of his age. He had done exceptionally well in all facets of his training. The mothers had pushed him much harder than most of the others, and tomorrow, he would be paraded among the wealthiest matrons of the queendom, to be sold like common livestock.

A normal slave sold between two and ten gold, about the same price as a cheap horse, while academy slaves sold anywhere from fifty on upward to a thousand gold. The highest price he had heard of in his years at the academy was slightly over two thousand gold, more than enough to buy a decent-sized farm. From his limited understanding, slaves were used as a status symbol by the nobles. As children, they would buy a slave and treat them like a new toy until the next one came along, then the slaves were either sold off or put to work, depending on their skills.

Mark hadn't worked hard for the sake of his mother, who had the option of letting him stay a free man, but in the hopes of gaining a high position in a noble's home, hopefully a kind one. If he had to be a slave, he would rather be one that worked in a lady's home, rather than one who worked in her fields. Mark also held on to a thin sliver of hope that he would have a chance to escape before he was branded. Though, from the stories he had heard, that was very unlikely.

A dark shadow passed over him, and he found himself staring into the eyes of Mother Elisa. She was a beautiful woman, with her slender body, narrow cobalt blue eyes, and dark brown hair. If only her attitude matched her appearance. She was his least favorite of the mothers. While most of the mothers were kind and understanding, Mother Elisa was hard like forged steel, and twice as cold. Mark quickly jumped to his feet and lowered his head. "Mother, how may I be of help to you?"

Though he dared not look up, he could feel Mother Elisa's eyes boring into him. "Follow me. Your mother is here to check on her investment."

Her tone was cold, but in it, he could detect a hint of compassion as well; that was something that unn-erved him far more than the knowledge of the imp-ending visit with his mother.

Mark followed Mother Elisa into the main building that stood in the center of the academy. After winding down a multitude of hallways, Mark found himself standing before the door that belonged to the matron of the academy. His body tightened, and his hands began to sweat as Mother Elisa knocked on the door. The light rap of her knuckles on the solid wood door sounded like a hammer to his ears. The thought of seeing the person, who had sentenced him to a life of slavery so many years ago, made his stomach feel as though it was tying itself in knots. An eternity seemed to slip by until the door opened, and Mother Elisa ushered him inside the room.

Having never been inside the matron's office before, Mark was amazed by the simple luxury of his surroundings. It was easily the nicest place he had ever seen. In the center of the room, the matron sat behind a large dark stained desk that was carved to look as if wood-colored roses were growing from it. In front of the desk, a woman, who could only be his mother, sat in an elegantly carved chair. Next to her was a younger girl, around the age of seven years, sitting in a less exquisite, but still elegantly carved chair. Mother Elisa indicated he was to sit in a lower, unadorned wooden chair with a small pad in the seat. Even though it was not nearly as nice as the others, this chair was still worlds more comfortable than what he was accustomed to.

The matron of the school stared at Mark. She was an elderly lady, slightly on the plump side, with salt-and-pepper hair. Her eyes seemed to bore into

Mark's soul. They seemed to hold secrets unknown to anyone else. The matron visited with the academy students often and had always been nice. She would reassure them with her soft and kind voice, but her eyes had always seemed cold and calculating.

"This is your son, Lady Marid. As my reports have informed you, Mark is one of the best students we have ever trained. He is an accomplished swordsman, archer, and scholar. If he brings less than two thousand gold pieces, I will be most surprised." As the matron spoke, Mark could see his mother's eyes light up.

As his mother rose from her chair, a large smile played across her face. She walked around Mark, her eyes studying him intently. Running her hand gently over his broad shoulders, her lips twisted into a thin smile. "You have made me very proud, son. At first, I thought you were nothing more than wasted effort, but you have proven me wrong."

Mark had always been a quiet boy. There was no advantage to be gained from angering the mothers. He always held his tongue in check and never caused trouble. Now, sitting in the same room with the woman who had abandoned him, and literally sold his life away, he could no longer hold his anger. "Never call me your son." His tone was hushed, holding only the barest hint of a biting edge.

As soon as the words left his mouth, he felt a sharp sting as his mother slapped him hard in the back of the head. "You ungrateful little brat! I have given you a chance to make something great of yourself, and you dare talk to me like some worthless whoreson!" Her words came out in a venomous tone, punctuated with continuous slaps.

Seeing nothing more coming from her son and no reproach from the matron, she let out a light

"Humph ..." and left the room, the little girl following quickly behind her. As soon as the two were well gone, the matron politely dismissed Mother Elisa, asking her to attend to her other duties. Mark was now alone in the room with the elderly lady.

The matron walked around her desk, slowly coming up to his side, lightly placing her hand on his shoulder. "Mark, did you know that my great-grand-mother started this school to fill the need for well-trained slaves? She saw a need and fulfilled it like any good merchant, even though she never truly believed in it. That is the reason we are on the border with Rane, where all my children have been born and are able to live in freedom. I myself agree with you. That woman has little or no right to call you her son, but don't let it make you bitter and ruin your chance to find yourself a good place in the world. You are a slave. That cannot be changed, but you can be a prized slave. You can be treated better than almost any other man in the whole queendom. It is not the best solution, but it is the best I can offer you."

Looking up, Mark noticed the matron's eyes no longer seemed cold. Instead, they radiated something akin to sympathy. Mark let out a heavy sigh as the truth of her words hit him fully. "I have known that for years, Matron, and have tried as hard as I could to assure myself a good place, but seeing her just broke something in me. I give you my apologies for my actions and I promise, I will be in my best form tomorrow." He could hear the catches in his voice and feel the tears that threatened to run from his eyes.

The matron gave a slight laugh. "Not to worry, son. I am not upset with you. More than once have I had to fight back words that I desperately wanted to tell some of these so-called mothers." She waved toward the doorway, smiling brightly. "Now, enjoy the rest of your day, and try your best not to let that woman bother you."

Mark made his way toward his dormitory, one of the five on campus. Even though high walls and guards surrounded it, Mark's life was fairly comfortable. The school gave privileges depending on your rank within the academy. Ranks 1 through 10 lived in the group dorms with little space, while ranks D and C lived in four main rooms, in the nicer private dorms. Then there were the very few A and B ranked students that the academy produced. They had rooms to themselves. These elite few had other benefits as well, such as better food and more free time. The best benefit, reserved only for A ranks like Mark, was that, for the most part, they were allowed to study whatever and whenever they wanted.

Once inside his room, he looked around at the Spartan conditions that were the majority of his world. His small bed, a desk covered in books, his practice sword, and a small chest containing a few changes of clothes were all that he owned. Picking up Paradox of Logic, Mark began reading and worked through some of the mental exercises that he found rewarding until he grew tired enough to sleep.

The next morning started with an extravagant feast for all those who would be sold at the auction. After a short word from the matron, their assignments for the day's challenges were handed out. The academy had sent out a full listing of available slaves with their overall ranking and skills to all the major buyers. Sword bouts were to be held between different stages of the auction for the bidders' entertainment.

There was a sparring bout held to display the relative skills of the first sixty-two slaves before they were auctioned. Two bouts were held with the twenty-one C and D ranks to not only display their skills, but also entertain the buyers. Lastly, the five A and B ranked students were to commence their bouts. An electric charge could be felt in the air as the final contest was announced. It would be Mark against Saru, the only other A ranked student currently up for sale. The young men were also informed that it was not uncommon for some of the more serious patrons to have their own fighters challenge the students.

After their meal, all the students were ushered to the waiting area, where arriving patrons could examine and speak with them before the start of the auction. It didn't take long for patrons to start filtering through the room.

Most of them stopped to speak with Mark, their questions quick, to the point, and utterly forgettable. The room was abuzz with excitement, though Mark couldn't seem to get himself as excited as many of the other students. Then the atmosphere changed suddenly. The room was silenced and emptied of patrons when heavily armed men marched through the door, placing them-selves throughout the room in positions that would allow them to quickly reach any student in case of trouble. After the initial shock of seeing the guards, Mark allowed himself to study them closer. He noticed the double moon crest on their chest plates and tattoos on their faces. He knew that either the queen or one of her representatives would soon be visiting. It was not a thought he relished.

Mark's curiosity was soon sated. From the corner of his eye, he could see a beautiful tall woman in a form-fitting dark blue dress. The color of her hair was the most fascinating thing about her. It was a deep crimson red and flowed around her shoulders, like a mantle of low burning flames. The sight of her brought more than a small reaction from his body. A few seconds later, he noticed a younger girl walking proudly next to the queen. She was almost like a miniature copy of the queen, but where the queen's face was demure and serious, the girl's was radiant. She looked a few years younger than Mark, not yet coming into womanhood, but she promised to blossom into a rare beauty.

The queen's walk through the room was slow as she stopped often to talk with the students, flipping through a thick set of parchments in her hands that held the names and specialties of each of the students. Her voice was soft but stern. She was someone who didn't just expect respect, but demanded it. It was the only time Mark could remember hearing anything that both excited him and scared him all at once.

The closer the queen got to him, the longer it seemed to take for her to move. Mark's hands were beginning to sweat, and his stomach was knotting up as she drew closer. Closing his eyes, he took a few deep breaths and started working through some of the mental exercises that he often used to calm his mind before a sparring match.

"You are Mark, the prize of this auction, with the highest rank possible in swordsmanship, archery, and mathematics and a good knowledge of politics, econo-mics, history, and military strategy. Quite impressive! Is there anything you do not excel at, young man?"

Opening his eyes, Mark saw the queen standing in front of him. "Yes, Your Majesty, I have had some trouble in the area of medical sciences," Mark responded coolly as he stared at the floor.

The princess let out a soft giggle. "Mother, he's cute! I want him for my guard," the little girl said, her voice light and melodious.

"We shall see, Maria. He will have to be properly tested, but no matter, I believe we can find a place within the palace for such a skilled slave." The queen spoke solemnly, with little emotion or inflection in her voice. Then it was over, as quickly and efficiently as they had appeared, the queen and her guards disappeared, leaving the room eerily silent until the next round of patrons began to make their way through the line of students.

The day passed quickly. Soon, they were led from the waiting area to the dining facility for a light midday meal, where they chatted about their prospective new owners. Mark spent most of this time trying to calm his nerves, his meeting with the queen still fresh on his mind.

Mark watched with disinterest as those he had known and studied with for the past eight years were sold off. They were chained and handed over to their new owners. In less than an hour, all the numbered students were sold. The patrons' energy and their emotions began to rise as the more desirable students were brought to the block. Patrons spent increasing amounts of gold to purchase the slaves of their choice. The day seemed to be passing in a blur, and Mark soon found himself standing in the arena for the bout that would start off the sale of the top students.

His opponent, Saru, was short, lithe, and very fast on his feet, but his attacks held little power behind them. Mark had sparred with him many times in the past and had never lost to the talented knife fighter. Saru had always considered Mark as his rival for the top position in the academy and had turned everything into a challenge to be won. Mark had only focused on his own studies and usually tried to shy away from Saru's taunts.

The battle began fiercely, with Saru coming at Mark and quickly striking with his two wooden practice blades simultaneously coming in at different angles. Mark let out a heavy sigh as he watched the attack pat-tern. He had hoped Saru wouldn't be so brash right at the onset of the fight and would allow both of them to display their strengths. But it seemed Saru wanted to end this quickly. That was one of Saru's main drawbacks; he always started with a flashy move. Outwardly, the move was good. With only one blade, Mark couldn't block both of Saru's swords, but he was skilled enough to know that he didn't have to.

Waiting until the last second, Mark dropped to the ground. Rolling around to Saru's right, he kicked, connecting with Saru's shin, knocking him off-balance. Wasting no time, Mark continued his roll, coming up behind his opponent. Saru, sensing his predicament, tried to dodge but chose the wrong side and took the full force of Mark's blow to his ribs, knocking him down. Saru's face was scornful as he looked up at Mark and the wooden blade at his neck. Mark stretched out his hand, but Saru knocked it aside, opting to spit a bit of blood on Mark's shoes instead.

The audience was unsettled, and Mark could hear complaints among the crowd. They had expected a more exciting battle between the top students. Mark could understand the disappointment. He had hoped to show off more of his skills than Saru had allowed. His and the patrons' wishes were soon to be answered as the queen stood, raising her hand high above her head.

"Not nearly enough to show us where your talents truly lie. I shall have the captain of my guard challenge you." Her statement was met with applause and eagerness as a burly man stepped toward the arena.

As the captain shed his armor and sword, he replaced it with a wooden practice blade of comparable size. Mark looked up at a man that towered over him by at least a foot with a body that looked as if it had been sculpted from granite. After giving a few practice swings, the huge warrior presented himself in front of Mark, who, unable to help himself, let out a loud gulp as he studied the massive figure in front of him.

Steeling his nerves, Mark raised his blade and reset his footing to match that of his new opponent. The battle started slowly, the guard taking measured strikes at Mark—testing his reaction—with each strike coming slightly faster than the last. Mark looked for an opening, no matter how small, as he parried the blows of his opponent. Soon, the attacks were coming so fast and hard that Mark was barely able to keep up. His hand was growing increasingly numb from the continuous impacts of sword on sword. He knew he was outmatched. The man in front of him didn't even look to be trying hard. If Mark was going to have any hope of even landing one solid blow, he would have to take a risk. But to get that chance, he was going to have to get some breathing room.

As the guard came with a strong underhand slice, Mark bounced on his toes, letting the force of the blow help carry him as he flipped backward. Mark landed hard on his back but ignored the pain and quickly rolled his shoulders, allowing him to jump up and backward to his feet. The guard gave an appraising look as Mark began slowly backing away, giving himself more room while keeping his sword up in case the guard decided to press the attack. The huge man seemed content with waiting for Mark to make his next move.

The guard made no move to close the distance. He simply stood, ready. It was as if he was waiting to see what Mark would do. Mark steeled his nerves, set his feet, and ran at the guard with everything he had. At the last moment, Mark went into a slide, slinging him-self right between the guard's legs. He had hoped to get a strike at the guard's exposed legs but was moving too fast and just didn't have the time or maneuverability to do it.

Coming up quickly, he struck but was disappointed as the captain of the guard deftly held his sword over his head, blocking the blow. The guard swung around, bringing his lead foot behind Mark's, and shoved him with his shoulder. His sword moved around at the same time, snapping at Mark's wrist, causing his blade to fly from his hand, and planting him hard in the dirt. Mark let out a silent stream of curses as he looked up at the victor, whose face remained indifferent as he held out his hand to the defeated, offering to help him to his feet.

Keeping his head lowered, Mark limped his way back to his position on the stage. Looking around the crowd as best he could, he noticed many of the ladies staring at him. They were chatting eagerly, ever so often pointing in his direction. Mark didn't know why, but the attention from the crowd made him feel lighter. It was impossible to keep a small smile from playing at the corner of his lips.

The first four students were sold for hefty purses, Saru going for 1,400 gold. Far too soon, Mark found himself standing on the auction block. His stomach knotted as the price got higher and higher. It quickly rose to over 2,000 gold pieces until, finally, the queen stood and made a bid of 3,500 gold pieces—an unheard-of amount for a slave. Mark could hear audible gasps from the audience at the amount, and he was quickly ushered offstage and chained, as was custom, until he was properly branded.

His chains were soon handed over to a much-too-eager princess. "Mother said you would be an early birthday present. She said I couldn't have you right away because you still have to be properly branded and trained for palace formalities, but soon, you'll be my private guard. Isn't it exciting?" The young princess rattled on so fast, giving him no chance to make an attempt at a reply.

Her voice, while lovely, caused his head to throb as he tried to keep up with the rapid pace at which she was speaking. His mind was in utter chaos and was more than slightly relieved when an elderly gentleman removed him from the princess and escorted him to a small carriage.

While they were walking, the old man chuckled. "The little miss has been begging for her mother to purchase you ever since they came out of the display room. Her pleads became even more persistent after your fight with Bren. Now we will be leaving soon," the old man said, letting out another small chuckle. "Well, as soon as the queen and her retinue prepare for travel. On the way back to the capital, you will ride and bunk with me so that I may begin your training in palace protocols. Don't get too excited. It will be boring and tedious, and it is mostly because the princess will most likely be badgering the queen until you are ready, so to save her a few headaches, we shall try and prepare you as fast as possible."

The old man opened the carriage door for Mark and helped him climb in. It was not an easy task seeing as he was chained. Once inside the carriage, the old man sat across from him and held out his hand, which Mark took absentmindedly. "First, introductions. I know who you are, Master Mark, and while I would love to give you the long introduction of my titles, I will forgo you that punishment. For now, you may call me Kris. Now before we begin, I would like to know if you have any questions so that I may clear up anything that might be troubling you."

"When will I be branded, sir? I'm not overly fond of chains."

"Sadly, you will have to wait until we reach the capital. The queen is quite insistent on your mark, and as custom dictates, since you are the property of the princess and not the queen, you will have a separate marking. When the princess chooses what her personal crest shall be, it will be tattooed on your forehead. I don't think it will take her long to choose. She seemed quite eager, if truth be told. I won't lie to you. It isn't a pleasant experience. Let's just hope the princess isn't too enthusiastic in her choosing."

The first day of travel was slow and uncomfortable. Every bump made his backside remember his sparring with Bren. His chains chafed at his wrists and ankles. Every few hours, they would stop, and Kris would help him outside so he could stretch and relieve himself. That night, they stayed at a nice inn, and Mark shared a room with the old servant, who contin-uously went over what would be expected of him and made him repeat what he was told until he could do it verbatim without conscious thought. After the day's grueling events, Mark was more than happy when the lights went off, and he could finally lie down to sleep in what was easily the nicest bed he had ever slept in.

The next day started with a hearty breakfast containing the largest collection of food he had ever seen. Though he still didn't want to give up hope and resign himself to being a slave, there was little chance of escape with the level of guards around him. If he had to be a slave, being one of the royal family didn't seem so bad.

The day continued much as the one before, with Kris going over the many palace procedures he would have to follow, focusing specifically on those surround-ding the princess. "Right now, you will be the only dedicated guard she has, but in the future, you will be required to train others as well. Back to the main point—your job is to not only provide her service but also be her confidant. Anything you see or hear while in her presence is confidential. Not even the queen is privy to them. If the choice arises, your honor and duty might send you to the headsman's block. That rarely happens as you will just be following protocol, but it has happened in the past."

Suddenly, while Kris was droning on, the carriage went out of control, jostling about and finally slamming to a stop, throwing Mark and the old man painfully onto the floor. Mark could hear voices outside yelling, "Protect the queen!" Soon, the sound of steel ringing on steel echoed outside. As quickly as he could, Mark got to his feet and went to help Kris, who was lying unmoving on the floor.

After a quick check, he breathed a sigh of relief. The old man was still alive, though unconscious with a nasty-looking bump on his skull. Once certain his companion was none the worse for wear, Mark kicked the carriage door open with his shackled legs—a feat that took several tries.

Outside, the fighting was fierce, and Mark could not see the queen's coach anywhere in sight. The royal guard had most likely gotten her away as fast as the bulky thing would move. Mark also did not see any of the royal guard, only the regular soldiers that traveled with her as an added escort. Useless, chained as he was, and no one paying much attention to him, Mark decided it prudent to hide in the nearby forest.

Once inside the dark canopy of the woods, Mark sat down beside a large oak tree and took stock of his situation. With no mark of ownership and as long as no one came looking for him before he could get his shackles off, he would be free. As a man, he wouldn't have many rights, but he would have his freedom. That alone was worth the entire world to him—a dream he never truly believed would come true.

As the noise died off, Mark nearly fainted when he heard the sounds of people moving toward him through the foliage. Soon, the sounds of talking could be heard in the distance. At first, the words were undeci-pherable, but after a few seconds, the brigands came close enough to be understood. "Dammit, Pete! We're shit-fire lucky the royal guard ran off with that coach! We'd been slaughtered if they had joined in the fight for any period of time. Did you see that one big 'un? He cut through Tom and Lewis like they weren't nuthin'," growled a rough voice.

"I hear ya, Chad. We lost near half our number with naught to show for it. Good fer 'im Lewis bought the farm, or I'd gut 'im myself! 'Twas his durn fool idea to go after 'em in the first place. Best we can do now is head back to camp and keep our heads down fer a good span."

Hearing footsteps on the forest floor, Mark realized they were headed in his direction! When they were close enough for him to hear their ragged breaths, his heart beat so hard he was sure they would hear it.

Fear held him in his concealed spot long after they were gone. He stayed, unmoving, until he noticed night was coming quickly. He knew he would have to find shelter, or his first night of freedom might be his last.

Walking through the dense forest was slow, his leg shackles leaving him little room for movement and often catching on roots and low-hanging branches. After a few hours, he could make out what appeared to be a crumbling house in the distance. As he got closer, Mark nearly tripped over a moss-covered stone wall. Looking around, he noticed it wasn't just a house but a small village lost to time. He made his way carefully toward the only building that looked as if it had survived the decay.

He couldn't tell what the building had been used for. It seemed deserted and left to the ravages of the elements. It was circular, so he figured it might have once been a grain silo. The top of the building had caved in, and the door was missing. He hoped the old structure would still offer some form of protection from the elements. Once inside, he noticed the building was bare, most likely picked over many times in the years it had sat deserted.

As he made his way across the floor, he could hear a soft groaning coming from the ground below him. Looking down at his feet, then back around the room, he could see no stairway leading down, and it didn't make sense to him to have a basement without a way to get to it. Suddenly, all his pondering was worthless as the floor gave way, dumping him into the room below.

Mark let out a loud yell as he landed hard on the floor. One of the stones from the floor above landed on his leg, sending additional pain through his already bruised and battered body. To make matters worse, his fall had stirred decades of dust that filled the room and now his lungs, causing him to cough uncontrollably.

Moving the stone from his leg, he carefully examined where it had landed. After he was sure it wasn't broken, he tried to stand, which was made extremely difficult by the shifting of the rubble under him.

Even after the dust began to settle, it was still too dark to make anything out in the room. Mark carefully made his way on his hands and knees until he found a clear spot on the floor and lay down. The air was slightly cold, and the floor was hard, but little of that seemed to matter at the moment. He had no energy left, so he pushed his worries and discomfort aside and let sleep overtake him.

Chapter II

Mark was awoken by a stray beam of sunlight that drifted across his face. Sitting up, he began to stretch. His body was wracked with aches and pains from the various beatings the day before had given him. Squinting and rubbing his eyes, his vision slowly began to clear as he surveyed his surroundings.

The walls were lined with what appeared to be bookshelves. In the center of the room stood what Mark was sure had once been a worktable. Now it was nothing more than a jumble of wood and stone. Looking up, he could see the hole he had fallen through. It wasn't too high, but with his shackles on, there was no way for him to crawl back outside. His only hope was to find some-thing to help him escape his bonds, or he would slowly die of hunger.

Mark made his way to the nearest bookshelf. Most of the books had long since rotted away to dust, and the ones left looked fragile. Amazingly, there were a few that still looked as if time hadn't touched them. After carefully making his way around the room, he found four books and a dagger that had survived through the years. Everything else he had found had fallen apart at a touch of his hand.

Sitting on the ground, Mark began to use the dagger to attempt to cut through his shackles. He held little hope for succeeding but was amazed to see the dagger was cutting through the hardened steel. It took quite a bit of effort, but within the span of an hour, the shackles lay discarded in the corner of the room.

Freed from his bonds, Mark carefully examined the dagger. He had never heard of a weapon that could cut steel. The hilt was silver, designed to look liked corded rope with two small sapphires at the ends of the crosspiece. Even more surprising, the blade was not marred in any way and still maintained a keen edge. The only answer he could think of was that it was magical. If that was true, it was worth a small fortune.

Excitement bubbled through him. Magic had been lost or, more to the point, destroyed during the Fae Wars when Emperor Tremon had declared war on any-thing of magical existence. For over a hundred years, the war raged on. Even after his death, the order of knights he had created roamed the land, killing mages and des-troying any relics of magic that were found. From his understanding, the Fae Wars was one of the reasons why Farlan was now a queendom.

Mark quickly grabbed and opened the first book. Disappointment filled him as he stared at the pages written in an unknown tongue. He was pleased to find the second book was written in his own language. He started reading and was soon absorbed in the volume.

It is the year twelve hundred and forty-six of the great empire. Emperor Tremon has declared war on all forms of magic. Since he could not bend us to his will, he has decided the empire would be better without our influence. In the past forty years, my brethren have been hunted down to near extinction, mostly by items of our own creation. My brethren have a plan to destroy all magical items used by the emperor, but the strain will most likely kill them. I was asked to help, but instead, I have hidden myself here in order to write this book in hopes that, someday, magic may once again be welcomed in the world.

First, you must know magic is present in all things in the energy of their essence. The ability to control and influence this energy is present in a limited number of humans. Like any skill, some are better equipped than others, and even the most talented require training to perfect their use of magic. But be warned—magic is not a cure-all and, in its own right, is a dangerous beast to wield. It will leave you dead if you do not take it seriously.

There are two main types of magic that manifest within an individual—internal and external. Internal magic is the ability to absorb and manipulate magic into your body. This can be used to make one faster and stronger, and for those mages of gift, it can even be used to shape-shift. External magic is the ability to mani-pulate magic in the outside world, using the elements of wind, water, earth, fire, energy, nature, light, and dark. Most mages tend to have a strong affinity with two or three of these elements. Few mages have mastery of four or more elements and are considered very rare. Of even greater rarity are those that can tap all eight elements equally. There are also sub-subcategories of skills that few mages show the skills for, such as magicsmiths, enchanters, and alchemists. All magicsmiths are ench-anters, but not all enchanters have the ability to man-ipulate metal, and alchemists are set aside from both.

Mark wiped the sweat from his hands on his dirty tunic. He couldn't believe it—a book about magic. It took great effort, and even then, he could barely keep his hands from shaking as he turned the page.

The next few pages contained abstract warnings regarding the ethical behavior that should be upheld as a mage. After searching for a bit, Mark found what he was looking for.

The way the flow of magic is accessed varies from mage to mage. Some see magic as a river and divert it to their will. Others see it as the wind and shape it. The most important revelation is that one must be able to visualize the flow of magic within the mind in order to bend it to their needs.

Find a comfortable spot, close your eyes, and meditate to find the flow of magic and shape it into a light. If you are an internal magic user, your abilities will cause your hand to glow. An external magic wielder will manifest a ball of light before them. At first, you may have to use a key phrase or gesture to help with your visualization. While these aids are not required, they can be useful to help your mind quickly visualize the spell you are performing and reduce the time and mental energy expended. Beware—it is advised that you use a dead language or one of your own devising. More than one mage has set his house ablaze by careless actions.

Mark sat the book down and quickly leafed through the remaining two. One was a book on herbs and potions, and the other was a book on the basics of enchanting. The book on enchantments made little sense to Mark, but his basic understanding was that it was an art of putting a permanent spell on an item. That en-chanted item could then be used by anyone. While the books were interesting, neither held his attention as other more important needs nagged at him.

Mark took one last look around the room but found nothing else of use. With no reason to stay in the dusty basement, he carefully climbed his way out and back into the daylight. Though he was eager to try his hand at magic, his first need was food as his stomach was already cramping, and his head was light.

Finding four fairly straight long sticks, he sharpened each to a point, fashioning crude spears. As he stealthily made his way through the forest, he spied two rabbits. Crouching, he readied the first spear. As the projectile left his grip, his spirits sank as both rabbits scampered off to safety. With his stomach cramping and about to give up hope on catching any live game, the sound of rolling water touched his ears.

After a short search, he found the source of the noise, a slow-moving stream. As he moved closer, Mark could see fish swimming in its shallow depths. Rolling up his tattered and dirty pant legs, Mark waded into the water.

No matter how he approached, every time he struck, the fish were well gone before his makeshift spear reached them. After countless hours, his frustration bubbled over, and Mark began stabbing wildly at the next fish that swam by. Cussing, Mark threw his spear into the water as hard as he could a short distance in front of him. To his amazement, the spear began to jump around wildly. Running over to his spear, he found a large fish impaled on its end. Laughing wildly, Mark collapsed in the water, tears of relief running freely from his eyes.

Once his hunger was sated, he found a nice quiet place and began to meditate. He envisioned the flow of magic as a dark red fog hanging around him. With his eyes closed, he held his right hand out in front of him. He forced the red fog to collect into a tight ball in the palm of his hand. Tiny beads of sweat started rolling down his face as he focused harder and harder on the image of the light. Suddenly, a slight tingling sensation shot through his body. Keeping his focus, he opened his eyes to see a dim red light hanging above his hand.

Surprised by his own success, Mark jumped up, and the light promptly disappeared. Reassured with his previous execution, he was able to bring the light back with little effort. This time, he envisioned the light as a soft blue glow. Laughing, Mark leaned back against a tree, amazed and delighted by the fact that he could do magic. What he could do as an external magic user was still a mystery to him, but he was determined to find out.

Mark read the book of magic late into the night. Using his mage light when the sun sat too low to provide sufficient light for him to read, whenever something in the book grabbed his attention, he would immediately try it out. As the book had instructed, he used key commands to make the casting of magic easier and quicker, but it wasn't as simple as saying a word. He had found the words had to have a clear association in his mind with the spell being cast.

The book had suggested using a dead language, but because Mark had no knowledge of such, he decided to alter the little-used Teran language for his key words. Instead of "luma" for light, he used "lumanare." After concentrating and casting the spell three times using the key word, he found he no longer needed to envision the mist. He needed only to focus and say the key word.

After making a fire and stunning a small frog that wandered into his camp, Mark's head started to throb, and he was having trouble holding his focus. Deciding it was time to retire for the night, he lay down and thought of what he would do in the morning. He wanted to make his way back to civilization, but he wasn't sure if he should practice his mage craft first or not.

His head hurting too much from overlong contemplation, he decided to let the morrow take care of itself. Laying his head back on the moss-covered ground, he closed his eyes and quickly drifted off into a pleasant and restful sleep.

The next morning, he was woken by the sound of something moving around his camp. Slowly, he opened his eyes to see a small fawn grazing nearby. Concen-trating, he focused on the paralyzing spell and released it. As soon as the spell was launched, Mark jumped up and grabbed his spear as he ran toward the fawn. He had not known how long the spell would last on a larger animal and was pleased when the fawn never moved so much as its tail.

He gave out a light chuckle. If only he had pra-cticed his magic before going hunting the day before, he would have been met with much better success. As his meal cooked, Mark began to read where he had left off the previous night.

One's ability to harness magic is not infinite, and there are limits to everyone's ability. Like a muscle, the more you use magic, the more your body will be able to handle. Still, there will be a point at which one will reach their full potential. It is best that you test your strength at least once every season. The easiest way to do this is to cast a spell and hold it until you can no longer hold your focus. As is known, different spells take more focus than others. I always advise using the same spell every year as well as using a spell with which you are comfortable. Use a spell just strong enough to have an effect, and hold it for an hour. Then double the spell's strength and repeat. Do not be disappointed if you cannot hold it for the full hour the first time. First-attempt success is rare. Rarer still is making it past the second doubling.

Mark knew that for the best measurement, he should perform the test without having preformed any magic, but he was eager to see how he measured with this test. He decided after he ate would be as good a time as any to do the exercise.

His belly stuffed with the leftover venison of the fawn, Mark wrapped the remains in leaves to carry with him for later. He took a seat on a comfortable moss-covered rock and prepared himself for the exercise. With little effort, the magical ball of fire sprung to life. Within half an hour, the front of his shirt was drenched in sweat, and his head was throbbing from the strain of main-taining the focus needed to maintain the spell. Not long after, Mark's focus faltered, and the spell fell apart, the flame dissipating into nothingness.

Collapsing on the ground, Mark found he couldn't move. His whole body ached as if he had taken a long run up a mountain. Even with the pain, a smile crept onto his face. If he understood the book correctly, his magical power was fairly strong. Too tired to move, Mark let his eyes close, taking the opportunity for a short nap.

Within a few days, Mark had read through the entire book of magic. He didn't understand a large portion of the book. It went into great detail about the different ways to use the elemental powers, but try as he might, he couldn't find the different flows around him. The book did offer a lot of ideas for spells, but most of them were simple or variations of ones he had already performed. He had read all the stories the academy had to offer on knights and magic, and he was sure that he had only scratched the surface of what he was able to do.

The fact that he would have to figure out the rest without guidance was daunting but, at the same time, refreshing. As far as he was concerned, he had no limits. Maybe he would even outstrip the mages that had come before.

Now that he had a fair understanding of magic, he decided to take another look at the book on enchanting. The book was fairly thick, but after flipping through it, he learned that it mostly contained information on metals, woods, gems, and crystals and advice on the best ways to use them with enchantments.

The basic idea was to put a spell on an item and have it collect and store magic to be used at a later time. One needed two basic things to enchant. A gem or crystal, referred to as the core, was to store the magic. The other item, referred to as the body, was to be of wood or metal. This item was to hold and direct the spells into the core.

He really wanted to try enchanting something, but without a core, it was impossible. He decided it was time to leave his little sanctuary and find his way back into the world. As a male, he knew he would be seen as a second-class citizen and unable to own land. He knew only the most basic jobs would be open to him, and if he wasn't careful, he would most likely find himself again as a slave or worse.

When his head began to throb, he switched to whittling on a large piece of oak that he had picked up in the forest in the attempt to make himself a new practice sword. He had worked tirelessly over the years to hone his skills, but the queen's guard had shown him he still had a long way to go, and he did not want to let the edge he had disappear.

After six days of working with the wood, the sword was finished. It was slightly off–balance, and the blade curved a little more than he wanted, but it was still better than nothing. With his new blade in hand, he went through his normal warm-up routine. Even though it had not been long since his last battle, he felt slow and sluggish.

While he practiced, a thought occurred to him. What if he could strengthen and sharpen the wooden sword with his magic? In a fight against an armed opponent, he would be at a disadvantage, and in a fight where he didn't want to draw attention to his abilities, it could be extremely useful.

Mark found a young tree that could easily be felled with few quick ax strokes and began focusing. He envisioned the magical mist wrapping itself around the blade of his sword, coming to a hair-thin edge, and then he swung the sword at the trunk of the tree. He felt only minimal resistance, and for a moment, he thought he had missed the mark in his haste. Suddenly, the tree fell over! Letting go of the spell, he looked down at his sword to reassure himself that it was still there. It had worked a lot better than he could have imagined.

The next day, he saw a small farm off in the distance and changed his direction toward it. He was running out of food and hoped he could replenish his stocks at the nearby farmhouse. He wasn't sure if it would work, but as he hadn't seen any game since leaving the forest, he had to try.

As he drew closer, he noticed the main house was much nicer than it had looked at first sight. It had dark brick walls instead of wood and a roof of tile instead of thatch. While it wasn't a mansion, the show of limited wealth caused Mark to hesitate. Anyone with money had power, and if they branded him, no one would take the side of a lone male. But with the little food he had, he had to risk it, so he forced himself to continue on, fingering his sword nervously as he knocked on the door.

A portly lady, easily in her late fifties, with dark brown hair answered the door. She looked him over, then let out a light chuckle. "Boy, what in the nine hells happened to you? You look as if someone strapped you to a horse and let it drag you over half the queendom!"

Mark stared blankly at the woman, his mouth hanging agape as he mentally kicked himself. Did he think he would just walk up and ask to trade labor for supplies? He knew he had to try something, but he couldn't think of an explanation for his current condition. Before he could think of anything, the woman gave him a scathing glare, and his mind shut down. "Well, come in. No reason for you to stand outside, catching flies all day."

Mark obediently followed the woman to a fairly large dining room with a massive solid wooden table that could easily feed fifteen people at the same time. When the woman disappeared from the room, he tried to think through his options.

What story would most likely allow him to continue on without landing him in trouble? Nothing came to mind, so he figured the best he could do was tell his story as honestly as he could while leaving off some of the facts. The lady reappeared and sat a small tray of smoked meat, cheeses, and bread in front of him. There was also a cold glass of juice that tasted sweet, with just the barest hint of a bitter undertone.

In an animalistic fashion, Mark gulped down huge bites and washed it down with the juice. Mark wasted no time tearing into the small feast that had been placed in front of him. Looking up, he noticed the woman was watching him with a large smile on her face. Swallowing a mouthful of food, he suddenly felt childish. "Thank you for the food, madam."

She let out a barking laugh. "No reason to call me madam. I would much prefer if you called me Joan as that is my name. As for your thanks, I would much rather hear why you have come to my farm half starved and looking as if you had been raised in the wilds."

"I'm not sure where to start. You see, I was just hired to work on a lady's estate and was in transport to the location when we were set upon by bandits. The bandits took little notice of me, so I ran into the woods. I was left without anything to my name and abandoned in unfamiliar territory. I started walking, hoping to find my way to my employer, and was about to give up hope when I came across this farm," Mark said, trying to make his voice sound as helpless as possible.

Joan looked at him, letting out another small laugh. "So basically, you were just sold into slavery, and in transport to your new master's home, you were set upon by robbers, and you ran away, got lost, and finally, made your way to my farm."

Mark nearly jumped out of his seat at the way she saw through his story and instinctively gripped the handle of his wooden sword anxiously.

Joan walked over to him, laying a gentle hand on his shoulder. "I wasn't born yesterday. The main hint was that no ladies hire someone that doesn't live close to their residence. Second, you left the road. If you hadn't run, you wouldn't be anywhere near my house. Now don't you fret. Not everyone believes that males should be traded like livestock. I promise you're safe as long as you're here. You have my word on it."

Mark let himself relax, hoping that she was telling the truth. After his meal, Joan brought him some worn but clean clothing and showed him to a washing area behind the house. The water was lukewarm from the sun and felt great on his tired and weary muscles. Seeing no one around, he let out a small spell to heat the water even more and lay back, closing his eyes and thoroughly enjoying the bath.

He was unsure how long he had lain in the bath, but he was stirred from his respite by a gruff voice. Looking up, he noticed a large bald older man with bulging muscles standing by the tub. "Well, boy, the wife is almost done with supper, so it's about time you dried yourself off and made your way back into the house. Make yourself quick about it. Don't need one of the girls spotting you half nude out here, do we?" The man's voice was deep but held a hint of laughter in it, making Mark smile as he quickly got out of the tub.

Inside the house, he was greeted by Joan and ushered to the dining room, where eleven others of varying ages already sat. He was placed between a girl with light blond hair that looked a few years older than him and a boy around his own age. The boy, whose name was Peter, was interested in Mark's practice sword and quickly began peppering him with questions.

Mark was amazed to learn they were all family members. George and Mercy were Joan and Robert's children, each married with kids of their own. They all lived and worked on the farm. They owned no slaves but allowed other families to work their land for a share of the profit from the crops they sold. As the meal was winding down, Joan began to inquire as to what his plans for the future were.

"I plan to make my way to the nearest city and find some work. First, I will have to get some provisions for the road. That's what brought me to your house. I was going to ask if there was some work to do in trade for food."

Robert gave Mark a calculating glance. "Well, planting season has just started, and we could use some help. We normally hire a few extra hands if they're available at a decent wage. There should be more than enough to help you on your way, but it will be some hard work, boy, and if you don't pull your weight, you'll find yourself out on your ass."

The room rang as Joan landed a heavy slap to the back of her husband's head. "I'm sure you will do just fine, Mark. Don't let my idiot of a husband bother you."

After dinner, Mark went outside, followed by Peter and Jonathan, a sandy-haired ten-year-old. The two boys watched as Mark went through his routine. The two quickly found sticks and tried to mimic Mark's movements with varying levels of success. When Mark finished, he heard clapping from behind him and turned to find George sitting in a wicker chair. "You look quite handy with that sword, kiddo! Where did you get it?"

"I made it, sir."

"Well, if you can see to make some for the boys there, I might see clear to finding an extra silver or two for you. I doubt me and my wife, Maggi, will hear the end of it until Peter has one of his own," George said, giving Mark a hardy slap on the back.

The next morning, Mark was awoken by Peter gently tapping on his arm. The sky was still dark, and sunrise still looked to be few hours away. As with dinner, breakfast was eaten with the whole family, and then everyone headed off to perform their jobs. Mark was led around by Peter, who showed him what had to be done. The work wasn't complicated, mostly plowing the fields. Through years of weapons practice, Mark had honed his body into sinewy muscles, and he responded well to the plowing. However, his hands were quickly covered in blisters from the rubbing of the plow's worn handles.

Clair, the young lady who had sat beside him at dinner the night before, brought his midday meal. She wore a light blue dress with pink flowers around the hem. Her blond hair was tied back behind her head, showing off her slightly plump face and her exotic light gray eyes. Mark thought her very pretty, not like the queen, but in a simple fashion. She laid out a small blanket and called for him to join her.

Mark dusted his pants off, took a seat across from Clair, and picked up one of the sandwiches she had set out. He noticed that her eyes never left him as she ate, her face turning a bright red when he caught her staring. At first, her reaction puzzled him until he remembered that he had taken his shirt off and hung it over a low branch a few hours before to keep from staining the only clothes he owned.

"I'm sorry. It was hot, and I didn't want …" His words trailed off as his face turned a bright red.

Clair let out a light giggle that made his face grow even hotter. "It's just that I've never seen anyone with their shirt off except my brothers, and none of them are quite so … defined."

An awkward silence filled the air until Clair let out a soft sigh. "Do you plan to leave as soon as the planting is finished? You know, Grandma wouldn't mind if you stayed around on the farm for some time. None of us would."

Though he had only been at the farm for a short time, he liked it. However, he craved adventure and wanted to see how far he could go in mastering his magic. He couldn't do that on this small farm no matter how tempting the offer was. "I can't stay. There are things I have to do. But I hope to come back and visit from time to time … if I can," he said sheepishly.

It took four days of working on the wooden swords at night before he was finished. He knew that they wouldn't last long if the boys hit anything hard, so he decided to take them into the small grove of trees that night and work his magic on them. He had learned that while his spell to sharpen the wood was an ethereal effect and not permanent, the one to strengthen it had been a permanent effect, making his sword almost as strong as stone and also adding a little weight to it. It would also give him a chance to work on a few new spells he had thought of while working on the farm.

Unlike at the academy, he was given free reign on the farm, and as long as he was awake in the early morning for work, no one said much about his comings and goings. Clair had found many chances to talk with him. Though most the conversations were short and brief, he began to enjoy the stolen time he had with her. As he walked into the grove, thoughts of what might happen if he decided to stay drifted though his mind.

Finding a secure area where no one could see him or what he was planning, Mark sat the two wooden swords down in front of him and began to concentrate. Though the spell was simple in its operation, simply telling the object to grow stronger sapped away a fair amount of strength from him and made his head throb lightly. Once he had completed his work on the swords, Mark picked out a patch of earth on which to try his new spell.

Using his dagger, he dug a small hole in the ground, placed a seed from one of the apples he had from his midday meal, and then covered it with loose dirt. Focusing, he pushed his magic into the seed, urging it to grow. His eyes soon began to blur, but he could see a sprout coming from in front of him. Then he felt something wet on his face but kept his focus as the tree was growing fast before his eyes. Then his focus shattered as he heard a scream from behind him.

Turning his head, he caught a glimpse of Clair running from the grove. She was running so fast, her blond hair appearing like a mane flaring behind her head. His legs gave out as he tried to get up. Staring at the ground, he noticed a few drops of blood striking the hard packed earth. Reaching up with an unsteady hand, he touched his nose and brought back blood-covered fingers. The book had warned him that pushing past his level could be fatal, but he had been too caught up in his spell to realize his life was draining away. Using one of the swords as a crutch, he made his way unsteadily to his feet.

The farmhouse could easily be seen from the edge of the grove, but the walk still took him a long time as he hobbled along like an old man. His fears mounted with each step, pondering what he would find when he got there.

He was met at the door by a concerned-looking Joan, who, upon seeing his condition, quickly called for Robert to carry him inside the house. He fought to explain what Clair had seen, but his words came out slurred and undecipherable.

Robert laid him softly in his bed, and Joan looked down on Mark with concern. "You rest. We'll talk about this tomorrow," she said, pulling the covers up around his shoulders. He didn't have the energy to argue and honestly didn't want to. With his head pounding, he doubted he would get much rest, but within a few minutes, he was sleeping soundly.

The next morning, he woke, surrounded by the whole family, everyone's face showing honest concern. After he pushed himself into a sitting position, Joan sat a bowl of broth in his lap. No one said anything as he ate. They just stood, waiting for him to finish. Putting his spoon down, Mark let out a heavy sigh. He knew these good people deserved the truth. After how they had treated him, anything else would be wrong.

"Last night," Mark said, pausing, unsure of the best way to approach the story, "Clair caught me performing magic. I took the wooden swords that I made for the boys to put a spell on them to keep them from breaking or marring easily. I also wanted to see if I could hasten the growth of a plant—an apple tree, to be exact. I overstretched myself, and this is the result." He then indicated his body with a flourish of his hand.

"Honestly, if Clair hadn't broken my concentration on the spell, I could have died. I'm sorry I didn't tell you before, but I didn't know how to approach the subject."

Joan laid her hand on his arm. "I can see that. Magic has been gone for some time, but you scared the young girl something fierce. She came in crying that you were possessed by a demon. I can't say I would have handled it any better seeing a tree sprout before my eyes. None of us were sure what to make of her ramblings. That and the state you returned in left a lot of questions to be answered, and magic would sure do that."

Doren, Mercy's husband, let out a harsh laugh, which earned him a scathing glare from Joan. "Right! Magic! You're telling me you have rediscovered the lost art and that's what sent my little girl running home in tears?"

Mark suspected they wouldn't believe it just on his word, but he was appreciative of the rest for not voicing their doubts. Bringing up his hand, he whispered, "Lumanare," and a bright, glowing blue orb sprung in his hand. Everyone let out gasps of excitement. Then the world went dark.

He woke to Joan holding a cloth to his nose, stemming the blood that was running freely. She wasn't looking at him, but at Doren. "The boy came back looking half dead, and you couldn't wait to see if he was telling the truth! I swear, sometimes I don't know what my daughter sees in you."

Mark tried to sit up but was quickly pushed back down by Joan. "You lay your hind end back down, mister. I'm upset with you enough as it is. That was stupid, tempting fate just to prove to that fool son-in-law of mine that you weren't lying. Dang men never stop to think past their own ego."

Though he knew Joan was mad, he couldn't help but laugh. "Thank you." The words didn't even begin convey the gratitude he felt for the old lady at the moment, but they were the only ones that came to mind. Lying back, he closed his eyes and let himself drift back off to sleep.

He woke again feeling much better. The sun was still up but hung low on the horizon. He had slept through the whole day, but at least his head had quit hurting. He sat up, and when no feeling of nausea assailed him, he risked standing up. Without any difficulty, he made his way down the stairs into the common room, where Joan and Mercy sat sewing.

Upon Mark entering the room, Mercy and Joan both smiled at him. "Feeling better now? I hope you're not pushing yourself," Joan said with a hint of concern.

"Much better, thank you. In fact, physically, I'm great. Though I don't think I should do any magic for the next few days," Mark replied, smiling.

Mercy gave him a shy smile. Like her daughter, she was very pretty, with gray eyes, but her hair was a light brown instead of blond. "You know, as a child, I always loved stories of mages. Do you think they could really call lightning from the sky and make rings that could make you invisible?" she asked sweetly.

Mark knew she meant to lighten the mood, but to him, it was a serious question. "I'm sure they could. I never tried to make lightning before. As for the ring, that is possible as well. If I had a crystal or gem, it might be possible for me to create one. That's one of the reasons I want to get to a larger city. So I can procure some cheap crystals and see if I have the ability to enchant."

As soon as the words were out of his mouth, Mercy shot up and ran out of the room in such haste that Mark thought he might have said something to upset her. Then just as quickly as she left, she reappeared, holding a box so tight in her hand her knuckles were turning white. She sat the box down in front of him. She quickly focused her intense gaze on him.

Opening the box, he was surprised to find it held about two dozen long thin crystals about the size of his index finger. "Do you think these will work?" she asked anxiously.

Mark was amazed! Though he wasn't sure of the cost, he knew the gems weren't cheap enough to just give away. "Are you sure? These must have cost at least a few gold pieces."

"Don't worry. They belonged to an ugly lamp my husband bought. I kept the crystals, though. But if it's not too much trouble, could you make something for me? It doesn't matter what, but I would love to have something magical." Her voice seemed almost pleading as if she didn't think he would. He didn't know why she thought that. If not for her, he wouldn't have been able to make anything yet.

"It would be my pleasure. Seems like a fair-enough trade to me. I will need some metal to set the crystals in if you want jewelry. Otherwise, it will have to be made of wood."

"We have plenty of broken tools, if you could use those somehow," Joan said casually, never looking up from her embroidery work.

"I'm sure I can find some way to make use of them!" Mark said, trying to hold back his excitement.

The next day, he returned to work on the fields. He still didn't see Clair and hoped she wasn't mad at him or, even worse, scared of him. After the evening meal, Mark went up to his bunk, carrying a broken sickle and the box of crystals. He knew doing magic too soon might be dangerous, but he felt great, and when he reached out and took hold of the flow of magic, he didn't feel any adverse effects.

The first task would be to trim the crystal into something more fitting. Closing his eyes, he focused on the crystal and began using magic to cut away the unneeded sections of crystal. Soon, he had a small spherical piece of crystal about the size of a pea. He repeated this and was able to get five such crystals out of one of the larger crystals.

Making a suitable ring out of the metal would be harder. He couldn't just cut away the unneeded area of metal like he had done with the crystal. He would have to bend and shape it. With much more effort, he was able to get three rings made before he started feeling his head begin the throb. Not wanting to push himself too far, he decided it was time to put his work aside for the night.

The next day, as soon as he was finished with his evening meal, he headed back to his room to continue his work. He quickly made two more rings and then sat a crystal in the center of each. Not feeling tired, he decided to push on. The first step would be making the crystal draw and store magic. He concentrated and focused on the gem, forcing his will on it. When he opened his eyes, the crystal looked the same, but he could feel it was drawing magic. The next part was harder. He had to make the body host the spell and react with the core when the key word was used.

The first five attempts failed, but he wasn't daunted. He continued to try different ways of seating the spell in the ring. After about an hour, he finally made it work. The solution was simple. He had to focus not only on the ring but also on the crystal when he envis-ioned the spell. But it took a light touch. One ring was completely useless—flickering on and off as the crystal stayed active. He also learned that when a ring and crystal were joined in an enchantment, they couldn't be separated without danger. The second he had tried to separate a crystal from a ring, the ring exploded in his hand, but the magic continued in the loosened crystal. Luckily for Mark, the ring quickly depleted itself, only singeing his fingers. But the ring and crystal were now completely useless.

After he finished the third ring, a soft knock came at his door. Setting aside what he was doing, Mark went over and opened the door. He was surprised to find Clair on the other side, looking down at the ground with her hands behind her back. Mark invited her in and sat back on his bed. Clair sat down timidly beside him.

After a long moment of awkward silence, Clair took his hand in her own. "I'm sorry. I was embarrassed after the other night, and I haven't been able to bring myself to talk to you. Mom has been begging me to make up with you. Dad isn't your biggest fan at the moment. Most likely because all Mom talks about is that you said you were going to make her a magical ring. Is it true? Are you really making my mom a magical ring?"

Mark let out a loud and heartfelt laugh, letting go of Clair's hand. At first, the tight smile on her face drop-ped, and a tear started to form at the corner of her eye. Then she saw what Mark was holding, a small ring. When he handed it to her, Clair's smile returned, much more confident this time. "Try it out. Just say, 'Lum-anare,' and it should work."

As soon as the words left her mouth, a soft glowing gold light hung in the air above the ring. Clair clapped happily, the little golden ball of light jerking back and forth in time with her hand. "How do I turn it off?" Clair asked, her voice holding more than a hint of awe.

"Just say the trigger word again," Mark said, trying to hold back another laugh.

Clair tried to return the ring, but Mark showed her the other two he had finished and said that one was for her. The gift earned him a kiss on the check, making Mark blush a deep crimson red. Mark soon found himself dragged back into the common room, where the family sat around, working on different things. Ever-yone's attention was soon fixed on him and Clair as she showed off her new ring.

Mark gave Joan and Mercy the other two rings, getting a hug and a squeal of delight from Mercy and a small smile and thanks from Joan. Mark stayed with everyone for a while, listening to stories, but soon made his way to bed, explaining that the enchanting had worn him out.

The next week went by quickly. He worked on the farm during the day and went to his room, where he and Clair would talk, at night. It was enjoyable, but the time for him to leave was looming ever nearer. The night after the seeding was finished, Clair came to his room with large tears streaming down her face.

Though it was hard to understand what she was saying through her wracking sobs, Mark understood that she didn't want him to leave. Joan and the rest had made it more than clear that he was welcome to stay as long as he wanted. He tried to comfort her, but he knew nothing he said short of promising to stay would work. Doren came and carried Clair to her room after she had soaked his shirt and cried herself to sleep.

That night, Mark decided it was time to leave. The longer he put it off, the harder it would be. He settled down into a fitful night of dreams of Clair crying. The next morning came quickly, and he felt no more rested than he had when he lay down. As he sat down at the breakfast table, he noticed Clair's eyes were swollen and red. It made his chest hurt, and he took a deep breath to steady his nerves. "I believe it's time for me to leave."

Everyone tried to talk him into staying for a few more days except Joan, who just sat silently. As soon as the meal was finished, everyone headed out to perform his or her daily chores. Each one gave him a hug or handshake as they left. Clair didn't say anything, just giving him a hug and a peck on the cheek.

"Before you leave, I have a few gifts for you. They're not just from me. Everyone pitched in. We all hoped you would stay, but I knew you wouldn't. We have been preparing for this day." Joan disappeared into the back room and returned holding a large leather traveling sack and a bedroll.

"The sack is from Robert. There is a small sack of coins inside. It's not much, mind you, but it also contains the coins George promised you for the kids' swords. I'll get together some food for your trip while you pack your things." The love and kindness in her voice nearly brought tears to his eyes.

Mark took the travel sack and headed to his room. Once inside, he opened it and found the bag of coins. It held fifteen silver coins and a few copper coins, nowhere near a fortune, but it was a start. He placed the last three long crystals into one of the pouches on the side of the sack and then added the many smaller crystal spheres into another pouch. He put nine rings into the sack.

He put the three rings he had made in anticipation of this day in his hand. One was a light ring. Another ring, when fully charged, allowed him use of the paralyzing spell three times before it was drained. The last ring held a shielding spell that would work for a minute and a half when fully charged. He had also carved himself a new sword and laid one of the long crystals into the hilt holding the spell to make the sword razor-sharp for almost half an hour.

With everything packed, Mark headed back down into the main room and waited for Joan to finish her preparations for him. He didn't have to wait long. She brought out a large bag and handed it to him. It was filled with smoked and salted meats that would last a long time on the road, along with some fresh fruit and sandwiches that he would have to eat sooner.

Joan gave him a hug. "Just so you know, you're welcome here anytime, Mark. You never asked, but the capital is only about an eight-day walk southeast of here. If you follow the small river down past the south grove, you will come to a road. Follow it, and you'll be in the capital in no time." When she pulled back from their hug, there were tears in her eyes.

Mark gave her the best smile that he could muster with tears teasing at his own eyes. "You have treated me like family, and I promise you I'll be back this way. If you ever need anything, find me, and I will do everything in my power to help."

Chapter III

Mark made his way, following the river as Joan had suggested. Things at the capital might get tricky, but he doubted he would ever see the queen or the princess. Even if he did, he doubted that they would remember him. Just to be safe, he figured it would be best to leave his old name behind.

The second night, as he was looking along the road for a place to camp, he spotted the faint flicker of a campfire in the distance. Wearily, he approached the small camp, trying his best to keep out of view. From the cover of the bushes, he could see two wagons, a large-looking coach, a handful of men, and a young lady in her early twenties with dark auburn hair. All of the men had a brand on their forehead, and many wore swords. The group didn't look overly inviting, so he decided it best to find his own camp farther away.

As he was about to turn around and make his way back to the road, one of the men, a large fellow with a thick black beard, raised a crossbow, aiming it where he crouched. "Don't know who you are, but best come out into the open, where we can all see you."

Mark raised his hands above his head and stepped into the dim light of the flickering campfire. "I don't mean any harm. I saw your light down the road and was just being cautious."

The young lady walked up behind the gruff warrior and placed a hand on the man's shoulder. "Car-mon, I doubt the young man poses much of a threat. No need to kill him just yet," she said sweetly, her voice soft and elegant. "Now, child, what has you traveling on this road?"

"Well, you see, I ran across a small treasure trove of magical items in a run-down ghost town in the middle of the woods a few days back. I decided to head to the capital to see what I could sell them for." He knew mentioning anything about magic was risky, but he was sure, with the aid of his magic, he could escape if the situation turned dangerous.

At his words, the young lady's light blue eyes went wide. "Magic, you say? You wouldn't mind showing me, would you?"

The way her eyes danced with greed made Mark take a step back toward the safety of the woods. App-arently sensing his agitation, she gave him a sweet smile. "Don't worry, child. I won't steal anything from you. I'm a respectable merchant from Rane. It's just that magic of even the most mundane sort is worth a fair amount of gold. In fact, we may be able to help out each other. I know that as a male here in Farlan, you're going to have a hard time getting anything near a good price for what you have."

Mark couldn't deny her reasoning. In fact, there was a fair chance the people in the capital would just take his treasures and throw him in jail until he disclosed how he came by the magic rings. Willing to take a chance, he brought out one of the light rings and activated it. There were varying responses from the group, ranging from surprise to awe, as the bright golden light appeared in thin air.

"Come with me. Business should be done in private and comfort," the lady whispered as she led him to the large coach. The coach turned out to be a rolling room of sorts, with soft fur covering its floor and walls, a small bed in the corner, and a short table in the center. The lady motioned for him to take a seat on the floor across from her at the table.

From one of the chests in the small room, the young lady pulled out a small jar along with two crystal glasses. "Before we begin our negotiations, there are a few things you must know. First, this room is soundproof. Anything said or done in here is forbidden to be spoken of outside. Just for future information, merchants from Rane take this very seriously.

"Second, it is customary to have a drink and converse before business is discussed. Where I'm from, we believe that whenever you do business with some-one, in a way, they become part of your family. Anyone caught stealing or misrepresenting his or her goods is executed. Now I won't cheat you, but if in the rare occurrence you are ever cheated by a merchant from Rane, get proof to another merchant, and it will be taken care of. Do you have any questions, my young friend?"

"I've never heard of merchants doing anything like that before," Mark said, trying unsuccessfully to keep the nervousness out of his voice.

The young lady let out a short laugh. "I would be surprised if you had! Merchants in your land have no honor in their trade … it's deplorable. There's good money in moving goods from Rane to Farlan. Now first, the introduction. I'm Monique of the Rose Trading Company."

"I'm …" He knew he couldn't use his real name. He needed a new one, but he hadn't figured out what to call himself. "Well, honestly, I don't have a name. I know I need one. If you would like to give me one, I would be more than happy to take it as my own."

Monique gave him a questioning glance, then softly rubbed her chin. "I shall give you a name, but if I ever hear you going by another, I shall consider it misre-presentation, and I've already explained the penalties for such an action. Is that agreeable?"

"Anything I say will be kept between us, correct?" Mark asked, his voice unsure and wavering.

"Yes. If you were to tell me you robbed and killed another Rane merchant for your goods, I would kill you, but no one would ever know the reason. As I said before, anything said in here is private … though I can't say it doesn't have consequence."

He thought about her statement and decided he would have to tell her the truth or risk making an enemy. Mark took a deep breath and hoped for the best. "My birth name is Mark. I was a member of the slave acad-emy. In transport to my master's home, we were att-acked, and I escaped. While lost in the woods, I came across a magic tome and taught myself the art of magic. The goods you will be buying were not found but were made by me. I need a new name for fear that my original masters might try and find me. I'm not all that pleased at the idea of becoming a slave after finally gaining a scent of freedom." Mark rushed his words, tangling them with each other. After he finished, he stared at the ground, waiting for Monique's response.

Monique was quiet for a long time. When Mark looked up, he noticed that she was rubbing her chin again, looking at him closely as if she were probing the very depths of his soul. "Well, that is quite the story. I have no reason to doubt you. If it's the truth, I will very much want to keep your secret as you could provide a profitable source of income for me. First off, your name. I think Thaddeus Torin will suit you well."

Monique brought out a small box and withdrew a silver ring with a gold face that was designed to look like a small wagon wheel with a rose where the hub should be. "Now let me explain. Torin is my family name. It is a rare gift to allow someone the use of one's family name, but if you're telling the truth, I think you may become a valuable asset to my family and me. Now if you accept, it is traditional for us to exchange gifts. Mine to you, as is custom, is our family ring. What you give me isn't as important, but the value of the gift expresses the value you put on joining my family."

He took a long, slow drink from his glass as he mulled over what Monique had said. Thaddeus wasn't a bad name, and having a surname couldn't hurt. The fact that the name was of Rane origin might dissuade people from trying to sell him into slavery so quickly.

Mark quickly dug out the only other ring in his pack that wasn't a light. "This is a shield ring. When you are in danger, just use the trigger command 'servo' to activate the protective shield. To deactivate it, repeat 'servo.' The shield will only last one minute and will then have to be recharged," Thaddeus said, exchanging rings with her.

Monique quickly put on the ring, not caring that it was made of steel and crystal. "I must admit, I normally pride myself in my patience, but this is too tempting. Would it be acceptable for us to go outside so I might try it out?"

As soon as they were outside, Monique called over an older gentleman named Collin. At first, Collin refused to hit her with anything. He eventually consented to hit her with small branch he had broken off a tree. Thaddeus was nervous. He hadn't had much opportunity to test the shields and only hoped they performed as he expected. As the branch descended, it suddenly rebounded with a light pop. Collin swung again, this time with much more force, and the branch snapped in half, causing the older man to stagger forward, off-balance from the momentum of the blow. Monique clapped happily, laughing as she tried to catch the poor man before he fell face-first into the dirt. Instead, she caused him to land hard onto her shield.

Still laughing, she pulled Thaddeus back into the coach. "Marvelous! Simply marvelous! I could easily sell this for a tidy sum. But as it is a gift, I think I shall wear it to the envy of all my peers. Now on to business. What do you currently have for sale, Thad?"

He pulled out the eight light rings he had made and placed them on the table. "All I have are light rings like I showed at your camp earlier. They are simple steel and crystal but will last for about five hours before nee-ding to be recharged. It takes about three days to fully recharge if the magic is completely depleted. The key word is the same for all of them, 'lumanare,' and they work in the same fashion as your shield ring."

Turning each one on and off, Monique looked them over closely. "They are not worth as much as the shield, but they will sell quickly. I can most likely get around a gold for one. I could get more if they were more fashionable." Monique continued to talk to herself out loud for a few minutes. "'I'll give you three gold for all eight."

Thad let out a soft gasp. Three gold was a lot of money for a few steel rings. He had let himself dream of getting two silver apiece. "Deal!"

Monique grabbed his hand in hers and gave it a hardy shake. She then pulled out an elegantly crafted dark wooden chest, counted out three gold coins, and placed them in a row on the table. "Next time, haggle a bit. I would have paid around four gold pieces for them. Let this be a learning experience for you."

He was so surprised with the amount of coin she had offered. He had never even considered countering her offer. As he mentally kicked himself, an idea came to him. "Are you headed to the capital?"

Monique gave him a teasing smile. "Yes, were you thinking of asking to travel with us?"

"I was thinking of it, yes. More importantly, I was thinking that I could make a few more rings on the way."

At the mention of the prospect of more magical items, Monique's eyes lit up and began to dance in much the same way they had looked when he had first seen her. It was slightly unnerving. "Do you have everything you need to do it? What can you make? We're carrying mostly furs and grain, but we might be able to come to an agreement," Monique rattled with a greedy gleam in her eyes.

He let out a small laugh of his own at the enthusiasm in her voice and the way she was suddenly tripping over her own words. A moment before, she had seemed so sure and confident. "I can do a fair amount, but the stronger the spell, the quicker the crystals will drain. If I had better-quality cores such as gems, diam-onds being the best, I could make much more powerful rings. Also, the better the body of the item, the better it is able to channel the spell, wasting less magic. Metals with few impurities, such as iron, gold, and silver, work better. Certain woods also work extremely well. In fact, lacewood and marblewood are supposedly the best."

Monique walked to the back of the small room and pulled a long chest from underneath the bed and began searching through it. After a few moments, she brought over a glistening silver-and-gold box with two nice garnets set in the lid. Her hands were shaking sligh-tly. "Can you use any of this?" Monique asked, opening the box up to reveal a large collection of jewelry.

Thad sent out his magic, testing the gems and metal. They weren't all great, but they were far better than what he had been using. "Yes, I could. If you want, as an extra gift, I could enchant your jewelry box so it won't open unless you want it to. You can even pick out the key word."

"That would be nice, but I don't want to sell you the jewelry. Instead, I would like to commission you to enchant them. We can discuss what spells I would like on them and what price it would cost to have it done. Will that be agreeable?" she inquired.

They spent long hours that night talking over what she wanted, and though he would be using her jewelry, he would be making a tidy profit. She even offered to pay him for the enchanting of the jewelry box, but he politely refused, saying it was merely a gift for his new sister, which made her glow.

It took six days before Thad could even see the capital in the distance. He didn't know what he expe-cted, but what he saw wasn't it. He could see a tall wall surrounding the city, but what surprised him were the many buildings that stood high above the walls. They were still miles away, allowing him to see the capital in its enormity. Hundreds of thousands of people could easily live within the walls without much trouble. He was nervous as he thought about the city. He kept telling himself that he would figure things out when he got there, but now everything was crushing down on him.

Brand, a nice man in his midtwenties with long raven black hair and a hawklike nose, sat down beside Thad at the small campfire he had built. Over the past few days, he had struck up a friendship with Brand, who he learned wasn't really Monique's slave but an emp-loyyee of the Rose Trading Company. The marks of ownership were painstakingly painted on with a dye and touched up every few days to cut down on problems while they were in Farlan.

"Something bothering you, Thad?" Brand said, poking at the fire with a thin stick.

Absentmindedly, he ran his hands through his hair that had grown slightly unruly over the past few weeks. Thad let out a heavy sigh. "I just don't know what I'm going to do when I finally reach the capital. I have been so fixated on reaching there that I never thought out what I was really going to do when I finally got there."

Brand gave him a serious look. "We will reach the capital fairly early tomorrow. I would suggest the first thing you do is procure you some clothes. After that, find a place to stay, and take it one day at a time. No reason to try and plan your life out before you know what is available."

It wasn't wisdom for the ages, but Brand's reassuring words did help ease some of the burden from his shoulders. He spent his last night talking with Brand, trading stories, and dreaming of what their futures might hold.

The next morning, Thad rode with Monique. They talked in the comfort of the coach. He had been able to enchant twelve pieces of jewelry, her money box, and the jewelry box. A few of the spells she wanted see-med useful, while others were less so. One ring simply glowed slightly, alternating colors every so often. Bec-ause the gem had been of good quality, the amount of magic used was negligible. Though the spell served no real purpose, it would last nearly indefinitely if she wanted.

A small bell rang inside the room, letting them know they were entering the city and that they would soon be coming to a stop. Monique took this as an indication to settle accounts. She pulled out her money box and turned the tiny key, causing the lid to spring open. "We haven't really agreed on a firm price for the work, but I think four gold pieces should more than cover it."

Thad laughed. "Four? You told me yourself that that the price of the jewelry went up greatly with the added magic. I think fifteen gold pieces would be more appropriate, and I still think you're still getting the better end of the deal."

Monique gave him a stern look. "Fifteen? I owned them to begin with. All you did was add a few decorations to them. You don't pay a gem cutter based on the value of the gem, but the work he has done. Five gold pieces."

Thad held his hand to his chest as if he had been wounded. "Added a few decorations? Wondrous magic and you call them mere decorations? My fair lady, you can find a gem cutter in almost any town, but how many mages do you know? For such a fair lady as yourself, I can go as low as twelve gold pieces."

Monique let her eyes go wide. "You have to take none of the risk. Not only did I purchase the items, but I also have to sell them before I can make a profit. After I pay you extorted prices, you will bankrupt me. If I must, I can go as high as five gold and ten silver pieces."

They went back and forth for a few minutes bef-ore finally settling on six gold and eight silver pieces. As soon as they shook hands, Monique broke into laughter, quickly followed by Thad. "Not bad. With more prac-tice, you might have gotten me up to ten gold pieces, maybe even more. It is a one-of-a-kind work, so it is hard to judge the market price, but I think I'll come out with a large profit from my investment. We will be in town for a few days before we head back through this way after the harvest season. I will be looking for you to see what you might have for sale."

Thad agreed to keep an eye out for her and to have some products available when she comes back through as long as he doesn't get chased out of the capital before then. Monique had warned him about the risks of a male trading, and he agreed. Sticking with someone he could trust was much more advisable.

The coach came to a stop, and Collin opened the door. They were in front of what Thad was sure was an inn. A signboard with two engraved doves and the wor-ds "Double Dove" hung above the entrance. Not having anywhere else in mind for his stay, Thad followed Monique and Collin into the building.

A busty blond-haired woman that looked to be in her midthirties greeted them shortly after they entered the inn. "Welcome to the Double Dove Inn," she said, smiling. "It will be two silver per room, a copper per horse. Food and drinks depend on what you order."

After Monique finished her business, Thad wal-ked up to the counter. "I would like a room, please."

As soon as the words were out of his mouth, the woman frowned down at him. "Thought you were with the merchants.Five silver a room, meals extra." Her voice had lost all of the charm it had held earlier, and her face turned into a sneer as he counted out the silver and placed it on the counter.

A young boy of about six years old led him to his room, where Thad tipped the boy two copper. The room looked nice, and the linens were clean, but at five silver a night, his money wouldn't last long. He would have to find someplace else quick, or he would be broke in a matter of weeks. With his few meager possessions sto-red in the small trunk at the foot of his bed, Thad stuffed his coin pouch into his jerkin, picked up his wooden sword, and headed back down the main hall. When he reached the desk, he inquired about a bath. After paying the one silver and being assured that his bath would be waiting for him when he returned from his outing in the city, he left the inn and headed toward the market district.

As far as he could see, the market district was lined with shops selling everything from cheap trinkets to jewelry so expensive it was ridiculous. He found a decent-looking clothing store and bought three new shirts—two dark blue and one nice light green. He also bought two new pairs of pants, a dark blue cloak with pockets lining the inside, and a nice money pouch. All told, it cost him twelve silver and eight copper for the clothes. Almost double what it should have cost, but as a male, there was little he could do about it.

Wrapping his new purchases in his cloak, he slung it over his shoulder and began looking for a someplace to purchase himself a sword, metal, and some more crystals or gems if they weren't too expensive. At one of the cheaper jewelry stores, he was able to purchase a large sack of crystals of varying sizes as well as a handful of garnets and about a pound of broken silver jewelry, costing him a total of one gold, four silver, and three copper. The lady was nice and didn't charge him too much more than what was reasonable. Then he found a blacksmith who let him buy two bars of steel for six silver.

With his materials for enchanting purchased, he made his way to a small weapons store on the edge of the market district. He had seen many others, but this one seemed the cheapest. While a good sword would be nice, he planned to use this one for a small experiment. If the experiment worked, even if the blade was of poor quality, it wouldn't matter. Besides, if he messed up, he wouldn't be out of much coin.

Inside the store was cluttered with weapons of every type, though most of them were rusty, broken, or marred in some fashion. He was surprised to find a man sitting casually behind the counter, whistling as he shar-pened a nasty-looking long dagger. "What can I do for you?" the man inquired, never turning to look at him.

"I'm looking for a short sword," Thad said, put-ting as much confidence as he could behind his voice.

The shopkeeper sat down the dagger he was sharpening and went to the back of the room. He rea-ppeared a few moments later, carrying a large assort-ment of short swords. The man displayed them on the counter and sat back down, returning to sharpening his dagger. Most of the swords were marred in one fashion or another. After a lot of consideration, he decided on a simple one with a small crack that ran the length of the blade.

The shopkeeper let out a slight chuckle at Thad's choice. After paying the five silver for the sword and another seven copper for a slightly used dark leather sh-eath and a small whetstone, he began to leave the store when the man put a hand on his shoulder. "Business is business, but I'm not about to send a young boy out without a warning. That sword you have there will break after the first few times it connects solidly with anything."

Thad assured the man it was more for show than anything else. He made his way back to the Double Dove Inn. As promised, there was a large tub filled with water and a small bar of lye soap waiting on him in his room. He quickly put away his packages and stripped down for a nice soak. The water was much colder than he expected, but the weather was warm, so it was oddly refreshing.

Once clean, he tried on a set of his new clothing. The pants were slightly longer than needed, but other than that, they fit well. The dark blue shirt fit snugly, but comfortably. Clean, refreshed, and dressed, he sat down and began to closely examine the sword. The crack wa-sn't all the way through, and with only a slight effort, he was able to bind it back together. With the sword whole, he began working the blade with the whetstone. The sw-ord was poorly made; the metal had been worked thin, and that also meant it could carry a very sharp edge even though it would dull quickly.

As he sat upon his bed, thinking of the best way to proceed with the enchantments on the sword, a light knock came at his door. He was pleasantly surprised to find Monique on the other side of the wooden portal. She was in a dark green dress with a low V cut that showed off her cleavage. The view got more than a small reaction from him.

"We have completed our business sooner than anticipated and will be leaving as soon as they open the gates in the morning. I thought I would take you out to dinner, if you're interested." Her voice was sultry, and it sent a shiver down his spine.

Giving her a smile, Thad grabbed his new cloak and took her arm. "It would be my pleasure."

Monique took him to a fancy-looking place that had large sculpted dragons standing outside the door. The main room was large with tables spaced out enough to give guests enough privacy. A petite young blonde greeted them and, at Monique's request, led them to one of the private rooms in the back. The room was simply a table surrounded by a large velvet bench, and while there wasn't a door, there was a heavy dark red curtain that closed off the room, providing a sense of privacy.

Taking his hand in her own and rubbing her hands across his knuckles, Monique said, "I must thank you. In all honesty, this is my first venture. My father was a well-known merchant but never had a business of his own. When he died, I sold the family home and bought myself a place in the merchants' guild and financed this trip. Before you and I met, I was making a small profit on this trip, but nothing that would come close to covering the debts I incurred. You changed that today. I made more than I ever thought was possible in one day."

He audibly gulped, earning a giggle from Monique. "I'm glad I could help."

Monique scooted closer to him and looked him in the eye. "I would like to offer you a share of the Rose Trading Company. There would be little money up fr-ont, but once the company is up and going—with us as the primary source of magical artifacts—in a few years, we will be rich."

"Sure ... I mean, we're family, right?" He tried to make himself sound confident, but he did a poor job of it.

"That we are! As soon as I make a trip down to Tremon, I'll make my way back up this way. Shouldn't be more than eight weeks, and I should be back. After that, I will make my way back to Freshmon in Rane. Then as soon as the passes clear, I will make my way back down this way. It will be almost a year before I can make that trip. At that time, if all goes well, we can open a branch of the Rose Trading Company here. How does that sound?"

He pretended to think about it as he ate. He had ordered roast lamb, and it was delicious, far better than the fare he was used to. Monique looked up at him often as she ate, her face switching from a seductive smile to a contemplative stare.

"Sounds good to me. I have plenty of materials to work with and should be able to get a large amount of items for you before you come back. Though I can't pro-mise I'll still be in the capital. I have learned that some-times unexpected things can happen."

Monique leaned over, giving him a kiss on the cheek.

"If that happens, just try and get a message to me. Before we leave in the morning, I'll get one of my guys to drop off a map to show you our expected route."

The rest of the evening was spent laughing, with Monique lightly touching his arm off and on. Once back in his room, Thad smiled as he thought of the evening. Monique was a lovely woman who excited him, but most importantly, she judged him based on who he was and what he could do, not his gender.

Early the next morning, Brand brought over a map as Monique had promised. His new friend bid

Thad farewell and ran off to meet up with the leaving caravan.

Once he was dressed, Thad made his way down to the main hall to pay for another night at the inn. He was greeted by the surly innkeeper, who looked none too happy to see him. "No, your friends are gone. I'll not have you stay another night at my inn. Take yourself over to the Horse Head Inn in the squatters' district."

With all his belongings in his sack, Thad made his way into the poor district of the town. After a short search, he found the Horse Head Inn. Inside, he inquired about a private room but was disappointed to learn that all they had was one large common room. Leaving the inn, he walked around town, looking for any place wh-ere he could practice his magic undisturbed.

He searched every inch of the squatter's district, but everything was jammed so close together he cou-ldn't find any place that offered even a hint of solitude. The sun was going down, so he decided it was time to make his way back to the Horse Head Inn and take up his search again in the morning.

His mind wandering, Thad walked right into a poorly dressed man with matted and dirty hair.

"What have we here? That's a nice-looking sack you're holding there. What do you think, boys? Should we see what our friend is carrying to make sure it isn't anything dangerous?"

Thad glanced around, noticing six others with the man in front of him. Thinking quickly, Thad kneed the man who had spoken in the crotch and ran back the way he came as fast as his legs could carry him. As lo-aded down as he was, the group behind him was gaining fast. He had to do something, or his life in the capital would be a very short one indeed. His panic peaked as he turned down a small alley and found himself trapped by a dead end. He backed into the corner, staying as quiet as possible, hoping that the mob would pass him by. He noticed a sewage drain and quickly dropped to his knees, pulling at the grate. The grate lifted free with a loud screech. Quickly replacing the grate, Thad could hear the men searching above but couldn't make out their muffled voices.

The smell, as he reached the bottom, made him gag. The sewer was larger than he expected. The system allowed waste to flow under the city, where bacteria decomposed it to nutrient-rich compost. Three times a year, the sewers were flooded, carrying the fertilizer into the farmlands south of the city. The ceiling of the sewer had a thick growth of moss that absorbed the smell. In the academy's history book, it was said that the sewer was built before the Fae Wars and had been completed thanks to the combined efforts of many imperial mages.

Thad made his way down the dark tunnels using his light ring to illuminate the damp, discolored walls. One by one, he checked each of the many branches off the main tunnel. While not the most desirable location, it did offer the one thing he needed—privacy. He found three suitable sites to make his new home. After car-efully considering all three, he decided on the small room below the school for highborn children.

Not only did it allow him privacy, but it wasn't far from the market district. The sewer port allowed him fairly easy access to the largest source of information in the queendom. Though he would have to break in at night and find a way to move around unseen, the sch-ool's library was too tempting to pass up.

Within hours, he had devised a shield that would protect his sanctuary when the sewer was flooded. Next, he conjured a few lights to help explore the library. Fin-ally, he imported moss from the area surrounding his homesite. The added moss filtered the air to the point where it was breathable.

Chapter IV

Within a short span of time, after making a few trips topside to purchase cleaning supplies and scented candles, Thad's new home was becoming more habitable. With nothing to keep him busy, he had spent most of his time reading through his books. The alchemy book was interesting, but he just couldn't understand most of it since he had not studied chemistry while at the academy; that subject was reserved for students who had shown potential in herbology and medicine. That made his urge to gain access to the school's library above him even greater, but first, he had to devise a spell that would allow him to go unseen. He had made great strides in that area, but nothing he tried worked well enough. He could make people not notice him, but it didn't work on everyone.

Other than his project to gain entry into the library, he had also come across the mention of the making of a staff. Unlike most of the enchantments he had sought, this one required the use of multiple cores and spells working in unison to allow a mage to cast strong spells with less power having to be drawn through him, thereby allowing him to last longer without mental fatigue. A staff's strength depended on the maker. As it absorbed magic, it would take on a semiconscious state, and the book hinted that while a staff would always work for its creator, it could reject a mage that it didn't find worthy of its use. It was an interesting idea, but if he made one, he wanted it to be made of the best materials, and for that, he needed to get his hands on a large piece of marblewood and some decent-sized gems.

He also kept a steady pace on creating magical rings and necklaces for Monique. Every day, he found he could go on longer and longer without the headaches. He also learned to spot the telltale signs so he could stop before he found himself in discomfort. He had placed his sword on the back burner and had not worked on it since coming to the sewer, but he knew he would have to finish it sooner or later.

He was running out of food and needed to make a run up into the market district for supplies. He also had a few other items he wanted to pick up so he could work on some new ideas. Grabbing his empty sacks and woo-den sword, he made his way down the tunnels toward the exit that led into a small alley at the edge of the squatter's district.

His first stop was the carpenters, where he got two small lengths of cedar about the size of his forearm. A quick stop at a roadside cart got him a mixture of apples and pears, then the shop he dreaded the most, the butcher. He had stopped by the day before while chec-king prices and had found them the most reasonable, despite the shopkeeper who eyed him like a piece of candy.

Walking into the butcher shop, he was greeted by an older woman easily in her mid to late sixties. "Hey, sweetling, did you come back to take me up on my offer? I'll teach you the trade and even keep your bed warm at night." As if to punctuate her statement, a large crash followed by a lot of yelling came from outside the store.

"No, Cathleen, I just need to get some smoked meat, maybe a few sausages, and a steak or two," Thad said, trying his best to keep his face calm.

She quickly packaged his order, wrapping them in a thick, heavy brown paper that he would later clean off and use for his notes. "Here you go. Only two silver for you, and if you reconsider my offer, you just come back, cutie."

Thad quickly dropped the money into her outstretched hand and placed his food into his sack, repositioned his other purchases, and left the shop quickly. Outside the shop was a mess. A carriage had been overturned, and people were gathered around, trying to get a look at the incident. Not overly interested in the affair, he made his way back toward his waiting grate and solitude.

Before he had traveled far into the squatter's district, he heard a girl's piercing scream. Though he had few reasons to help out the fairer sex, his thoughts kept drifting back to Clair, Joan, and Monique. Thad jogged toward the direction of the scream to find four of the men who had chased him into the sewer trying to tie up a young girl. She looked familiar, but he couldn't spare the time to remember where he might have seen her. Pulling his practice sword from its makeshift holder strapped to his side, Thad yelled at the men to let the girl go. Two of the men turned toward him, one holding a small dagger and the other a rusted bastard sword. Thad cleared his mind and triggered the enchantment on his sword.

The man with the sword attacked first, with a swing toward his midsection. Thad moved his weapon in position to block the blow and was happy when he saw the man's eyes go wide as his sword was nearly cut in two. His other attacker came in quickly, leaving Thad no time to capitalize on the other's shock. He dodged the first two dagger strikes, then went on the attack as the other man began to try and circle around behind him. Knowing he was running out of time, he pushed the attacker, putting the dagger wielder off-balance, then, with an overhead strike, severed the man's arm right above the elbow. He then quickly turned on his other assailant, who was coming in with a vicious overhand blow. Thad was barely able to get his sword up in time to keep his head from being split open like a ripe melon. While he had been able to block the strike, the blade of his attacker's sword broke off, hitting him in the face and cutting a deep gash on the right side of his head. Thad kicked out with his right foot at the other man's knee and was rewarded with a sickening crunch. The man's cries were cut short as Thad's sword followed, quickly removing his head from his body.

Turning, he expected to see one or both of the remaining men preparing to attack him. He found one holding the girl, whose hands and feet were bound, and the other holding a knife to her throat. "Stop, boy. Come any closer or follow us, and I'll cut her pretty little throat," the man holding the knife said, his voice filled with both fear and desperation.

Thad slowly hooked his sword back to his waist and held his hands straight out, causing the two men to visibly relax. With two quick words, he activated his paralyzing ring, freezing both men where they stood, and calmly walked forward. He removed the knife from the thug's hand and quickly cut the girl's bonds, grabbed her hand, and ran. Thad never looked back, running straight toward the small alley that would lead back to safety.

The young girl followed him without a word into the sewer, quietly sobbing. Without thinking, he called a spear of light to his hand. Once back in the safety of his home, he gave her a waterskin and a small piece of smoked pork. Looking at her closely, he figured she was around eleven years old, and her dress, though slightly ripped, appeared expensive. Then he swore inwardly as he remembered where he had seen her.

"My name is Thaddeus, and as soon as it's quieted down outside, I'll get you home." He tried making his voice reassuring, silently hoping she didn't recognize him.

"Maria. My name is Maria. I live in the castle." She looked up at him, her smile looking odd with her eyes red and puffy. "How did you make those men stop? Your ring flashed, then they just quit moving."

Thad let go of another string of silent curses; he had let the princess see him use magic. "Just a trick, my lady."

She didn't say anything right away, so he took the chance to take off his ring and replace it with one of his new rings made of silver, with two garnet cores. It was made a little differently as it had two trigger words, one to paralyze an individual and one to paralyze a group within a fifty-foot circle around him. The group spell could be used once every three days, and the individual spell could be used about eight times before it was exhausted. He also replaced his shield ring with a new one that could last up to five minutes.

Turning his attention back to the princess, he noticed she was now standing with a haughty look. "Not only the guards but the light from your hand and the lights in this room. That wasn't just a trick, and I dem-and to know how you did that right now." The fear was gone from her voice, replaced by a commanding tone.

Thad tried to think of an excuse, but nothing came to mind—nothing he thought the girl would buy—so he decided to at least limit the damage done.

"They're magic rings I dug up in an ancient tower in the woods." He casually tossed her one of the light rings he had made the day before. "You can have this one. Just say 'lumanare' to turn it on and off."

She looked skeptical but put on the ring. It automatically resized itself to her finger. He was proud of that achievement; it took a few extra hours of work but was well worth it. Holding out her hand, she examined the ring, then triggered it, her face turning into one of awe. "What else do you have?"

Rubbing the sides of his head, he let out a heavy sigh. "Just the one that stops people and the light rings, though I plan to make a trip back and see what else I can find."

Thad was happy that instead of asking any more questions, the little princess sat, playing with the mag-ical light, moving her hand around fast, and watching mystified as the light followed her hand. But the peace only lasted as long as the light did. As soon as the magic ran out, so did the silence. "Why did it go out?"

Thad held out his hand for the ring, and the princess hesitantly passed it to him. He used the key word to turn it off. "Magic isn't infinite, Maria. The crystal here pulls it from around us and stores it until it is needed. Once that magic is used up, it needs time to restore itself. Give it a few days. It will be fully recharged," Thad explained, handing the ring back to the wide-eyed princess.

Looking at her now, he had to admit that although she hadn't hit her womanhood yet, she was still quite cute. With her long curly red hair slightly disheveled, her emerald green eyes, and her ripped gossamer gown showing off the soft pale skin of her shoulder, Thad had no doubt that she would bloom into a beautiful woman. Catching him staring, she furrowed her brow and drew her lips in a tight line. "What?"

"I thought it was about time to get you home," he said, quickly getting to his feet.

He took the young princess to one of the exits at the edge of the town. After checking to make sure no one was around, he handed her his cloak, which she took without comment and wrapped tightly around herself with the hood pulled up. The only thing that could be seen was her shoes. As soon as the palace gates were in view, he leaned down. "You should be safe from here." He spoke quietly so as not to draw unwanted attention.

As he turned to leave, Maria's hand grasped his arm tightly. Turning, he noticed she had tears in her eyes. "Please don't leave me alone." Her words came out pleadingly. Against his better judgment, he allowed the princess to drag him up to the main gate, where two large and heavily armed guards greeted them with cros-sbows. Before he could object, the princess unwrapped herself from the folds of his cloak, handing it back to him gently. He took the cloak and went to make his exit but was foiled as he was soon surrounded by dozens of palace guards.

Within seconds, he was thrown to the ground roughly and kicked numerous times until the princess stepped between him and the female guard who was accosting him. "This man saved me. I don't think my mother would approve of him being treated so. Even if he is a male." She then turned and quickly made her way into the palace, while he was helped up and led at swordpoint to a small but opulently decorated room.

While he waited, a bath and change of clothes were prepared for him. The bath was welcome as he had not been afforded the chance to take one since he had been at the Double Dove Inn. The clothes, while elegant, seemed a bit overdone to him. The doublet was a dark red, with a lighter red trim, and the pants were dyed as dark as night, with a silver trim running down both sides and across the midsection. There was also a deep black pair of boots with silver buckles that fit him well eno-ugh, if a tad too big. To top it off, his hair was pulled back with a silver string into a tight ponytail that pulled at his wound.

Even after the long bath and tedious dressing and pampering by the horde of slaves that kept checking and double-checking him to make sure he was ready, he still had plenty of time for his own worries to make their way to his mind. By the time he was brought to stand before the gold-trimmed double doors leading to the audience chambers, he had his nerves strung tight.

He was marched into the room, flanked on each side by three royal guards. The queen sat on a large dark wooden throne decorated in gold leaf. She was beautiful, wearing a sheer white gown with small diamonds sewn all over it, making her sparkle. The princess, now wearing a dark green dress that looked nice, if a bit extravagant, sat on a smaller throne to the queen's right. Remembering the proper protocols, he readjusted his sight to the floor and went down to his knees, placing his head upon the floor.

"You may rise." The queen's voice was soft yet stern; she waited for him to get to his feet before contin-uing. "I see. So you made your way to the capital, young man. The name was Mark, if I remember correctly."

Thad tried to keep the fear from his face. "Your Majesty, my name is Thaddeus Torin."

The queen gave out a short laugh. "My young man, do you think I spend that kind of money and don't remember the occasion? Honestly, I thought you would have taken up with the bandits that attacked us. I am glad to see that is not the case, but now that you are back with us, you will have to be properly branded, of course. I suppose we can forgo the punishment for escaping seeing that you saved my daughter."

Thad bowed low again, silently triggering the group paralyzing spell of his ring. The room stood silent as everyone but Thad was frozen in time like a statue. He went into a crouching position in case any other thre-ats presented themselves. "I humbly apologize, Your Majesty. I was hoping it wouldn't come to this. Don't worry, it will only last for a short time." He could see the queen's eyes shaking in rage. "But I won't be a slave."

Thad braced himself, preparing the most powerful paralyzing spell he could muster. His head began throbbing at the sheer amount of magic pouring into him. Opening the door, he had to brace himself against the frame as a multihued array of colors danced on the edge of his vision. Outside, everyone was frozen in place. As he made his way to the main corridor that led outside, a loud alarm rang out throughout the palace.

Everyone was in a panic, so no one stopped him until he reached the iron gates, where four guards barred his path. "Stop!" one of the guards yelled, leveling a spear at his chest. Thad obediently stopped and raised his hands above his head, cursing silently to himself. Having little choice, he started a spell and was happy that, unlike in storybooks, he didn't have to wave his hands in silly circles and use long incantations. He could hear the guard in front of him telling him something, but in his current semimeditative state, he couldn't unde-rstand what. The guard turned to one of his companions and said something. The other guard drew his sword and approached him. Hoping the spell was strong enough, Thad let loose.

With a loud roar, the ground below the gates exploded, sending dirt and metal in all directions. Thad had barely got his shield in place in time before the shock wave washed over him. The guards, not being so lucky, were thrown down to the ground, and a stray length of iron had impaled the one with the spear. Thad felt bad for the guard, but his body was already feeling the effects from his overuse of magic.

He wasn't sure how, but one moment, he was staggering through the streets, and the next, he was lying down on the hard floor of his home, with a small red-headed form leaning over him. He panicked, sitting up and backing against the wall. Looking around, he noticed he was home and not in the palace dungeons. "What are you doing here?"

Ignoring him, the princess set aside the washcloth she held in her hand and began making a plate of food out of his stores. "You know, Mother is quite livid. She has every guard and soldier searching the town for you. They are to detain you only, though. She won't admit it, but she was quite impressed with you. More importantly, though, you lied to me."

He futilely tried to stand, finally giving up as the princess walked over and handed him the plate of food. "First, you lied about your name, then about being a mage. Don't try to lie again. I may be young, but I'm not stupid."

"I didn't lie about my name. It really is Thaddeus. I left my old name behind. As for the magic, I'm sorry, but I won't be a slave."

The princess put her hands on her hips and tried making a stern face that looked more cute than fierce. "I know. I tried reasoning with Mother. Even if they dra-gged you back, we would never be able to control you without your cooperation. You already proved you could have easily killed us all yesterday."

An uncomfortable silence filled the room until he let out a heavy sigh. "Guess it's time for me to leave Arith." He could follow the route Monique had left him in hopes of meeting up with her, or he could make his way to Rane and wait on her.

"NO!" the princess shouted. "I won't tell her where you are at, and I can bring you some food from the palace." Maria's voice started to break, and a tear ran down her cheek. "I promise I'll get Mother to grant you your freedom. Just, please, don't leave."

To say he was stunned was an understatement. He couldn't understand why the princess cared if he left or not. In truth, he wasn't sure why a host of guards weren't already clasping him in chains. He could ask, but for some reason, that felt wrong too. After finally giving up trying to understand the princess's motives, he just smiled. "OK, I'll stay around, but I would like to know how you got down here without anyone following you."

Maria ducked her head, her face turning a bright red. "There is a secret passage into the sewers in the basement of the palace. It's so the royal family can escape in case the palace is ever under siege."

It made sense to him, though he was sure he had searched every inch of the sewer. Shrugging his sho-ulder, he took another bite from his plate. The princess nattered on about how boring the palace was, sneaking in questions about his magic from time to time. He answered the questions as best he could, but when he mentioned that most people, once trained, could learn magic, she became insistent that he show her.

"Why won't you teach me?" she huffed after the third time he politely refused her request.

He really didn't want to tell her, but it didn't seem she was going to give him much of a choice. "From my understanding, you shouldn't train in magic until you have matured."

At first, the princess's face was confused, then as understanding of what he meant sunk in, her face reddened. "Oh."

After making him promise to teach her as soon as she was "ready," she left, happily promising to come back as soon as she could with food and supplies to last him until things settled down.

Maria was nothing like what he thought a princess would be like. She was outspoken, demanding, manipulative, and self-important, but also kind. Lying back down, he found himself oddly looking forward to her next visit.

The princess visited every day; her visits were always erratic, sometimes staying for hours, other times just for a few minutes. She always brought the latest news, and the past few days, all she had talked about was the big party her mother was planning for her eleventh birthday. On her last visit, she had let him know that, with all the commotion over the party, she wouldn't be able to visit for a while, but also that the hunt for him had dwindled down to nothing. The queen was sure that he had left the city and was well on his way out of the queendom.

The party was still four days away, and he wanted to do something special for the princess. He had an idea for a gift, but he was out of materials to enchant with, so he decided it was time to risk a trip into town.

The fresh air felt great compared to the dank air of the sewers. His first stop was at a shop, where he purchased a small wooden box with a hinged lid. He then went to the jewelry store, where he bought a small bar of silver, a small diamond, two emeralds, three rubies, and a handful of amethysts, costing him a little over four gold.

Knowing he also needed more for Monique, he stopped by the blacksmith, getting a few bars of steel, then before heading back home, he stopped at the small trinket shop, buying enough crystals to last him a long time, as well as a few glass orbs.

Back in his lair, Thad emptied his coin pouch into his hands. Three gold, a few silver, and a handful of iron pennies. At the rate he was going through gold, he would be broke in no time. Resigning himself to cut down on his spending, he began working on the princess's present.

The box was simple but made of a dark purple wood that was very catching to the eye. Using a small amount of steel, he made settings for the gems and arranged them in the box. The rubies and emeralds circled the diamond, and lastly, the amethysts circled the rest. Once everything was set out, he began focusing on the silver bar, forcing it to become paper-thin.

Magically manipulating metal was always draining and took the majority of his energy when enchanting. His head was starting to throb as he placed the silver sheet on top of the gems and concentrated, allowing it to melt around them. He covered the entire bottom of the box while still allowing the gems to be seen. With nothing else to do while he waited for his mind to rest, he grabbed a block of wood and his dagger and began whittling.

It took him two days to complete the box, but he was happy with the finished product. Unlike his other items, the box didn't use a key command but was keyed so that when the lid was opened, it triggered the magic. While the spells used were simple, he was very proud of the core design. The rubies and emeralds fed magic to the amethysts, and the diamond was set to regulate the overall magic flow. When the lid opened, small lights of a myriad of colors filled the area, dancing around in a random pattern.

Now he just had to find a way to move around the palace unnoticed. It wasn't the first time he had tried to find a way to go unnoticed, and he had many ideas, but he didn't have time to try them all. He needed som-ething that would last a long time. Getting in and out of the palace was easy since he had followed Maria to the secret passage. There would be a lot of people at the party, but few of them male, so he would stick out like a sore thumb. Maybe an illusion to make him look female would work. He had thought of using it before but had never got around to doing it. Illusions didn't take a lot of magic, and even without a ring, as long as he kept his concentration up, he could keep it going for hours. But keeping one's focus while moving around was hard, and if anyone talked to him, he wouldn't really be able to respond properly. Illusions took a vast amount of focus, especially one on the scale he was thinking. Every detail had to be held in his mind. One small misstep and the spell would fall apart.

He had been working on an idea to allow him to use his spells fast with minimal focus. He had an idea, but it required a very detailed enchantment, using himself as the core. Taking up one small tile of wood covered in a thick casing of steel, he began to work. The enchantment book had been specific that not everyone could enchant—it was an inborn talent in which a person could infuse magic with objects and bend them to their will. So most of his enchantments only took as much magical energy as casting the spell placed on the item. Aside from what he expended to shape the metal, all he was doing was making the item memorize the spell. This time, not only did the item have to memorize the spell, but it had to take its magic from him, which was much more complex, but if it worked, he could cast his spells the same way his rings did, quickly and continuously. That is, until he passed out from the strain.

After four hours of work, it was finished. Since he planned to make more of them for his different spells, he carved a small design onto the tile. In the stories he read, mages always used runes for their spells, so he considered that it would be as good a name as any for his new toy. His new rune still needed to be tested, and what better place than the city?

With his disguise on, Thad made his way to the Double Dove Inn with a letter for Monique in his hand. The letter was only a small reason for his visit, the main one being testing his disguise on the innkeeper. The woman he had remembered as mean and cold greeted him warmly, asking him if he would like a room. He politely declined, handing her the letter along with three copper coins to keep the letter until Monique was able to make her way back into town.

Having lived off smoked meat and fruit for the past few weeks, his stomach grumbled at the smell permeating throughout the inn. He had little planned for the rest of the day, so he took a seat at a table and was promptly greeted by a young sandy-haired waitress. "What can I get for you, miss?"

"What is the special for the evening?" Thad's throat itched as he tried to keep his tone soft and feminine.

The waitress beamed happily at him. "We have a great beef stew served along with a fresh loaf of bread."

"That sounds fine. I would also like a bottle of cold juice to go with my meal, please." He had thought about ordering wine but didn't want to mix his magic with the effects of alcohol.

The food was brought out quickly and was good, but it made his stomach ache since it was a fair amount richer than his usual fare. Well fed, Thad made his way through the market, stopping and chatting with various vendors. The experience was much different than his other visits to the market. There were no sneers; vendors called out to him, offering him fair prices; and everyone was smiling at him. If nothing else, his disguise would save him a fair amount of coin next time he needed supplies.

Wanting to test how long he could hold the spell before the exhaustion started to get to him, he decided to see if they would let him in the school. He had pur-posely made his illusion that of a fifteen-year-old girl, thinking it would allow him the most freedom of movement.

He was happy that no one stopped him as he entered the school, having thought of no excuse as to why he was there. The library was easy enough to find thanks to little plaques on the wall pointing the way to various places of interest within the school.

The library was huge, easily twice the size of that of the academy's. He found the section on history and ran his finger across the books' spines as he read the titles. All the books were organized by date, so it didn't take him long to find the few books on the Fae Wars and imperial history.

He knew his time would be running out soon as he had already been in his disguise for over two hours, so he tried to make a mental note of where the books were located and began to make his way back to the en-trance in the squatter's district. Shortly before reaching the sewer grate, his head started to throb slightly, letting him know that his magic was starting to take its toll.

Looking around to make sure no one was around, he dropped his disguise, smiling. It had worked per-fectly. With any luck, he would be able to make his way into the palace with little trouble. Walking back to his lair, he began to think about what he should do next. He still wanted to make himself a staff, but for that, he needed a lot more gold than he had. Maybe he could make something that functioned in the same manner as a staff. The staff worked in much the same manner as his runes, with the exception that it also worked as a conduit for the magic to lessen the strain of casting as well as strengthening the spells. If he were to fuse cores the same way he did the runes, he could tap them and cha-nnel them into the different runes, allowing him to use them to augment his own strength. He wasn't sure if it would work, but the theory seemed sound. The only downside was that crystals wouldn't be able to handle enough magic to make them worthwhile, and gems were expensive. If he wanted to continue on with his experiments, he needed more gold.

The next day, he donned his disguise and once again made his way to the market. The party was later that night, and while he could make an illusionary dress, everything he performed with magic increased the str-ain, so if he bought one, it would increase the amount of time he could hold the spell for before he started to feel its effects.

He had brought along two of his magic lights, made to look like candles that gave off a bright blue light, to sell. While he had promised Monique to limit how many he sold, he needed gold, and it was the only thing he had of any value. He went to the most expe-nsive-looking jewelry store in the market. Inside, the lady behind the counter gave him a questioning look. What was he doing there? Her eyes asked the question before her mouth could. "I'm from the Rose Trading Company and am here to see if you would like to buy some magical items we just got in."

The lady's eyes widened as soon as the words were out of his mouth. "Ah yes, Lady Monique sold us a few of her magical trinkets when she was last in town." The lady stopped as if waiting for him to say something, then cleared her throat. "Yes, well, let's have a look."

Thad placed the two magical candles on the counter, turning each of them off and on. The lady, not one to be fooled, did the same. "I don't know where your company is getting these, but if you could get me some silver candles like these, I would be willing to pay a hefty sum of gold. As for these, I think five gold api-ece would be a fair price."

"I apologize, miss, but five gold is not near eno-ugh. If I had the time, I would sit here and haggle with you to my heart's content, but I don't. Eight gold is my firm asking price, and I still think you are getting the better deal. I would normally try and get ten each, but as I said, I am in a hurry," Thad said, making his voice as bored-sounding as he could.

The shopkeeper let out a slight laugh. "Here I was, hoping you were some young kid on her first trip. All right, eight gold each, but next time, you owe me a good haggling."

Sixteen gold richer, Thad made his way to the dressmaker. Inside, the store was like nothing he had ever seen before. In all the shops he went to for clothing, everything had been neatly paced on shelves, but here, lengths of fabric hung all over the place. Making his way through the jungle of fabric, he finally reached the counter, where an old salt-and-pepper-haired lady sat. She was busy sewing what Thad figured was some sort of dress decoration, so he politely cleared his throat.

"Can I help you, dear?" she said, looking up from what she was working on.

"Yes, I just made it into town, and I need a dress for the party tonight as everything I have is not suitable for the occasion," Thad said, trying to make his face look abashed.

"Follow me, dear. I'm sure we can find something suitable," the old lady said as she headed toward the back corner of the store. Luckily, there was a small changing room since his illusion didn't cover some of the more private areas of the female anatomy. After five different dresses, he finally decided on a dark green dress with way too much frill for his taste, but the seam-stress had assured him that it would be perfect for the party. While he was there, he also ordered five other dresses to be made for him for daily wear. If he was going to have to spend time as a woman, he might as well have more than one outfit for the occasion.

Not wanting to overly stress himself before the party tonight, he quickly made his way back to his home in the sewer. Even after the dress and new outfits, he still had over fourteen gold.

The time for the party came around fast, and he soon found himself making his way through the secret passage into the palace. The palace was abuzz with excitement as he came out of a small sliding section of wall that led to an unfamiliar hallway. Following the other partygoers with his wrapped present under his arm, he was soon standing in the grand hall that was so packed it was hard to move around without bumping into someone. Each person made their way to where the princess sat, handing her their gifts and making polite conversation for a few seconds as two guards, one on each side, searched the crowd for potential threats.

Shrugging his shoulders, he got in line to present the princess with his gift. While waiting, he started going through names that he could use as an introd-uction, finally settling on stealing Clair's name for the night. The wait to see the princess was almost half an hour, but it was well worth it. She looked stunning with her hair done up, wearing a light pink dress that seemed to float around her like a cloud. She kept a smile on her face, but it never seemed to reach her eyes. If anything, it appeared to him that she was undeniably bored.

Once in front of her, he bowed deeply, holding the gift out in front of him. She took the gift and opened the box, trying to make herself look enthused; she didn't have to pretend once the myriad of colored lights sprung into the air to the gasps of the other partygoers. While everyone else was watching the dancing lights, the pri-ncess looked at him, and he gave her a sly wink, wig-ling his ringed hand at her. She got the hint and gave him a bright smile.

The princess closed the box. "It is a fine and wondrous gift. I would like to know whom to thank and why," she asked as if the question had been rehearsed. Then again, it most likely had been.

"I am Clair of the Rose Trading Company, and we have recently started trading here in Farlan. We just wanted to show our appreciation to you and yours for the fine reception we have received."

"Yes, I have heard of the Rose Trading Company. They unloaded a fair amount of magical items in the capital the last time they came through. I would be most pleased to learn where they are getting access to such valuable artifacts." Thad nearly jumped up and ran when he heard the voice of the queen. "Though I sent a message to your headquarters in Rane, I doubted it would be answered so quickly and with such fanfare."

Thad bowed lower, touching his head to the ground. "I was unaware of such a missive, Your Majesty. I was dispatched sometime ago and only reached the city yesterday. I was surprised I was even allowed inside the palace. The original plan was for me to arrive days ago and petition for an audience, but due to unforeseen occurrences, I was delayed. I most humbly apologize."

"And where has your company been able to get all of these magical devices? I must say, it has me intrigued." The queen's voice was kind, but Thad could feel the underlying thoughts behind her words. She suspected that her runaway slave and the Rose

Trading Company were working together, and she was right.

"I don't rightly know, Your Majesty. The company is fairly new, and I have not worked for them for long. There is a lot of gossip among the other members that the mistress of the house found a treasure trove of magical items or that she has rediscovered magic herself, but in all honesty, I do not know the truth of these rumors, and just for speaking them, I could well lose my place within the company." Thad let some of his fear slip into his voice, hoping that the queen would see him as a simple messenger.

"When you can get a message to your superiors, I suggest you tell them I would love to have an official meeting to discuss the potential for some contracts. Now enjoy yourself. I am sure you and my daughter will get along well, especially considering the gift you have brought her, but first, I need to have a word with her." The queen signaled for Maria to follow her.

Maria returned, quickly flashing him a dazzling smile; she waved her hand, asking him to sit beside her as a chair was brought for him. "Mother wants me to get to know you. I am advised that building a friendship with you might be advantageous to the queendom," the princess whispered as soon as he was seated.

As soon as the rest of the visitors had presented their gifts, they all retreated to the dining area, where the princess sat to his left and another young girl with light brown hair was seated to his right. Throughout the meal, he casually chatted with both girls. The brown-haired girl asked the majority of the questions about the gift he had brought the princess. As the meal was winding down, his head began to throb. He had already been inside the palace for slightly over two hours, and he knew it was time for him to make his exit but couldn't think of a way to do that as he was under the uncomfortable eye of the queen.

After the meal was over, everyone returned to the grand hall, mingling around as a group of musicians played a variety of music. The second he and the princess were given a moment of peace, he leaned down and told her he couldn't hold up his disguise much longer. Having spent a lot of time around him, she understood what he meant. "How much longer can you keep it up? Everyone should be breaking off now to their own engagements, and it wouldn't be unseemly for you to leave at that time. Shouldn't be more than another half hour?"

Thad rubbed his hand across his brow, trying to ease the slight throbbing of his head. "I should be able to hold that long, but I'm going to be hurting in the morning," he said, letting out a light chuckle so as not to worry the princess.

Just as the princess had said, the party quickly started to wind down, and people began moving away. While Farlan wasn't the biggest land, it still took a great deal of time to travel from holding to holding, and gath-erings like this were great opportunities for the highborn to make arrangements. From what he had learned at the academy, the school was much the same; while all the nobles could easily afford private tutoring, Farlan's nobles sent their children to school so they could mingle with others of the peerage and make valuable future contacts. Many other counties also sent some of their nobles to the school, much for the same reason, but in all fairness, the school was one of the best available.

With the party dying down, Thad made his way to the front gate, not wanting to take the chance of getting caught using the secret passage. No one stopped or questioned him on his way out of the palace grounds, and he soon found his way back to his lair.

Chapter V

The next morning, he woke to the expected headache. The night before had gone well; he only hoped that Monique wouldn't be put out with him for using the company name during his visit to the palace. Sitting up, he was reminded of his overuse of magic the night before as his vision blurred. He wanted to get to work on his idea of augmenting his own magic, but he knew he should wait at least a day before he started on the project. With nothing else to do, he began carving out more small wooden tiles. He could just use wood or metal, but he discovered that if he used two different bodies—one holding the spell and the other linked to him—it made using them much easier and wasted less magic.

Using a thick stick of charcoal and one of the many pieces of brown butcher paper, he began working on a diagram for his staff. He wanted it to be made of marblewood, and it needed to be about six feet long. If he worked it the same way he had the music box, using a large diamond as the core focus and other gems as subcores, it would greatly increase its potential. If he could get his staff made along with his rune necklace, he would be incredibly dangerous. The staff would increase his power while reducing the strain, and the necklace would allow him to cast spells with reduced focus and feed him saved magic. If he made both with the other in his mind, he might even be able to make them more effective.

To test his theory, he planned to make a weak version of each before sinking a large amount of gold and time into the full project. He already had a large selection of magical items for Monique, and it was still weeks before she would be coming back through the capital. He had other projects in the works too, like making an offensive ring. He had tried using metal, but no matter how well made, he got magical feedback from the spell, which, with a fire spell, resulted in him getting a bad burn. He had tried a lightning enchantment with a wood body, but it blew apart, nearly taking off one of his fingers with it. He had a workable idea for fire. He would make a stone ring with a metal coating on the outside. He had yet to come up with a workable idea for lightning or his explosive spells. Physical effects like his paralyzing spell were easy since metal and wood didn't have a moving body to affect.

Early the next morning, he donned his disguise and headed straight for the carpenter's shop. He was pleased to find that due to an order for a marblewood table, they had some leftover wood available they had yet to put to use. The longest block was seven by one by one, much bigger than he needed, but with the superior magical conduit ability of the wood, he was sure he could find a use for the extra. The wood alone cost him a fair amount of his coin, but that had been expected given the rarity of the wood.

Inside the jewelry store he had frequently visited, the familiar shopkeeper greeted him. "I am in market for a large diamond as well as some other fair-sized gems," Thad said, trying his best to mimic the princess's ent-itled demeanor. The shopkeeper said little but brought out a large selection of gems of every shape and size from the back room. The largest diamond was the size of a large grape. "How much?"

The lady fidgeted for a moment, waiting for more information on what he wanted to know the price of; seeing nothing forthcoming, she started giving the prices of all the gems.

"The large diamond there is twelve gold, the smaller ones range from one gold to eight gold, the rubies and emeralds range from two silver to three gold, the amethysts and garnets range from a silver to a gold, and the rest vary on cost. If one strikes your eye, just ask, and I'll quote you a price, my lady."

Looking through the assortment of gems, a dark blue one about the size of plum, with a thin streak of white through its middle, stood out. Probing it with his magic, he found that it held the equivalent potential of a ruby. "May I ask what this is called?"

"That is called a cat's-eye gem. We have plenty of them in the western sapphire mines. I get them cheap since most people view them as imperfections, but in the right setting, they're still very fetching. One that size, I would sell you for five silver. The smaller ones are much cheaper."

After a few moments of quiet deliberation, he finally decided on the large diamond and five plum-sized, twenty-five grape-sized, and fifty pea-sized cat's-eye gems. He couldn't believe his luck. The cat's-eye gems were cheap and extremely suitable for his needs. Only sapphires, emeralds, and diamonds were better, and the first two not by much.

His coin pouch was almost empty, containing only a single gold and a few silver, so he made his way back home. He would need to sell some more of his items, but that could wait a few days. He still had plenty of food, and the items he was currently working on would keep him busy for quite some time. The marblewood was heavy, and he began to tire quickly. Trying to get it into the sewer without just dropping it down the hole was near impossible.

Once back in his lair, he immediately went to work on the staff. After an hour of cutting at the wood—first with his magic, then with his magical dagger—he understood where it got its name. Not only did the wood look like marble, but it was as hard as stone as well. After nearly six hours of steady work, he finally had the staff looking the way he desired. The main shaft of the staff was sleek and only about as thick as the hilt of a sword, gradually getting thicker until it ended with a spherical top.

Setting the staff aside, he flexed his aching arms. Even with the magically enchanted blade, he had to put a lot of strength behind it to cut the wood. He still had to cut out the sections where the gems would go, but that could wait for another day. He still needed to test out his theories before he finished his staff.

He picked up a small wooden staff he had made. It was only about two feet long and was adorned with a host of crystals. All it was waiting for were the spells to make it function, so he went straight to work. First, he linked himself to the miniature staff. Then one by one, he linked the ten smaller crystals to the bigger one. The staff worked in the reverse fashion of his normal spells. It collected magic into the smaller gems and sent it to the larger one, amplifying it and focusing whatever spell he was casting.

He didn't know how long he sat there, but when his eyes focused on his surroundings, he noticed that the princess sat cross-legged in front of him. He tried to speak, but his voice came out as more of a harsh whi-sper. Trying to move, he was suddenly aware of the massive throbbing in his skull and cramps in his arms and legs.

"Oh great, I was starting to get bored staring at you. It's not that you're bad to look at, but after a while, it grows old," the princess said haughtily.

He tried to rise, but his legs gave out, and he slammed headfirst into the floor, getting a gasp from the princess, who rushed over to him. She helped him into a sitting position using the wall of the room to brace his back. She quickly got him a skin of water, forcing the water down his parched throat. "Are you OK? What happened?" Her voice, which was slightly displeased a few minutes ago, was now full of concern.

"I let myself get drawn too deep into what I was working on. I'm not even sure how long I was out. I sta-rted working on it the night after our party." His voice still sounded hoarse, and every syllable spoken made his head feel as if it was being ripped in two.

"The party was three days ago," the princess said, giving him a worried look. "Stay right there. I'll be back shortly, and I swear, if you so much as move an inch, I'll beat you with a whip." As soon as the words were out of her mouth, the little princess darted out of the room. He chuckled slightly as he heard her footsteps echoing throughout the sewer. As soon as the princess was gone, he closed his eyes and let himself drift off to sleep.

He was awoken a short time later by a gentle tugging at his arm. Opening his eyes, he let out a soft groan as the princess pushed something into his hands. Taking a sip, he found that it was a cup of warm broth. It was rich, but very good. He was about to tell her that he wasn't an invalid yet but immediately thought better of it. As soon as he finished the broth, she forced him to drink another glass of water. As soon as he finished the water, they talked for a bit, but he kept drifting off to sleep in the middle of their conversation.

The next time he woke, his body was still sore, and the princess was gone. He felt bad about falling asleep during her visit, but he was sure she understood. He laughed as he thought of her last visit. He decided her caring side was cute as well. His headache was gone, though he hadn't expected it to last long since he had used very little magic on the staff. All the effort had been the intricate intertwining connections he had made to link the different crystals.

Thad picked up his miniature staff and placed it in his lap, then grabbed a necklace that held four crystals and three tiles that had already been engraved with runes and spells. Not wanting to stress himself, he made a mental note to take a stop after every few connections. He was happy that he only had to connect the four cry-stals with each other, with the main crystal, and with himself. It still took him over eight hours to finish, with two stops to eat, stretch, and relieve himself.

Shortly after he was finished, the princess, who was none too happy that he had been performing magic again, graced him with her presence. "If I find you nearly dead again, I'm going to drag you in front of my mother, clapped in irons, so you can take a nice long reflective rest in the dungeon."

"I was more careful this time. As I told you, I'm still new to magic, and it's not like I have someone to tell me what I should or shouldn't do. It's all hit or miss." She didn't take his explanation too well and chewed on his ear for a long time. He thought about antagonizing her a little more since she was cute when her hackles were up. In fact, she was always cute, he mused.

After her tirade was over, she sat down heavily next to him with a slight humph. "So what are you working yourself to death over anyway?"

Needing little reason to brag about his newest project, he started to excitedly explain what he was working on. After a few minutes of him speaking, the princess held up her hand, stopping him. "Please, keep it simple. You're giving me a headache."

"Sorry," Thad said, blushing. "The staff will allow me to strengthen my spells, while the necklace will allow me to draw on their strength to keep from draining myself so fast. There's a lot more to it, but that's the quick answer. If they work right, I'll finish the real staff and necklace. First, I'm going to have to get more silver as well as a silver necklace to attach them to."

"Oh, oh!" the princess said excitedly. "I just remembered—I thought of a way for you to gain a bit of goodwill with Mother. There is a large group of bandits wreaking havoc all over the queendom. They are demanding that all slaves be freed and men be given the same status as women within the queendom. Their message I can sympathize with, but their methods are ruthless. They are killing and attacking everyone on the road and killing those that refuse to join them. If you were to bring them down and maybe return the tax money stolen, it would buy you a lot of goodwill not only with Mother but with the other peerage who won't have to send out their tax men again."

Thad had been well schooled in economics and understood that if the slave system were abolished overnight, it would destroy Farlan's economy. The only way to move forward would be to slowly reduce the country's dependence on slave labor. As for making men equal, he could get behind that, but wanton slau-ghter was not the way to achieve your goals. "Once I finish my staff and a few other things, I'll see what I can do. If they're as ruthless as you say, I'll see to their des-truction." He spoke clearly but left the hanging question of what he would do if they weren't bloodthirsty killers.

As soon as the princess left, he went to one of the other small rooms in the sewers that he used to test any of his new ideas after he had accidentally set fire to his makeshift bed. First, he tested the rune for fire. It was made of stone, steel, and wood. He focused his magic through the staff, and a huge torrent of flames shot from the miniature staff. He tried each rune in turn and continued casting until his head began to throb. Even with the miniature staff and necklace made with cheap components, his casting ability and strength had nearly doubled.

Next, he pulled one of the glass balls he had purchased sometime back and began forcing magical energy to fill it. Unlike the gems, the ball started to glow a light red color. It grew darker as more magic was poured into it. Once it was a dark crimson red, he backed out of the room and threw the ball against the far wall as he took cover in the sewer main corridor. A loud explosion echoed throughout the sewers, making his ears ring with a high-pitched whine. Peeking back into the room, he let out a low whistle as he surveyed the damage. A fair-sized chunk of the wall had been blown apart, exposing the clay beyond. It had worked a lot better than he had expected. He knew from his failed experiments that when a core holding magic was broken, it violently exploded. Breaking a gem usually took quite a bit of effort, especially since he took steps during the enchantment process to make them near indestructible.

After three trips to the market, the sale of three more of his magical items, and six days of work, his staff and rune necklace were done, and he was ready to track down the bandits that had been terrorizing the roads.

He wore his disguise as he left the capital but dropped it as soon as he was alone outside the walls. He found a quiet place and sat down, unrolling the map the princess had given him of the queendom with all the information she had on the attacks marked on it. The bandits had started in the north and worked their way into the south. Their last two attacks were around Avael. He would have to travel east to Shiel, then south to reach Avael at a fast pace. He could be there in nine days or so. If he had a horse, he could make it in less, but even after selling some of his magical items, he only had a little over twenty gold to last him on this trip, and he needed to conserve what he could. His main fear was not getting back to the capital in time to meet up with Monique, but she would be traveling to Avael and Shiel on her way back to the capital, so if he was lucky, he would meet up with her along the way.

It took three days for him to reach Shiel; it wasn't nearly as big as the capital but was still a fair size. Wearing his disguise, he inquired about the bandits. He learned from a passing caravan that they had been spotted a few days' ride to the south, near the crossroads to Avael. Tired and weary from days of sleeping on the open road, he went to the nearest inn and ordered a room and a bath.

With his staff, it was easy to stay in disguise, but as soon as his bath was brought up and the slaves carr-ying it left, he dropped it and let himself relax as the hot water massaged his road-weary muscles. As soon as he was washed, he donned his disguise once more and went down to the common room to eat and listen to the gossip.

When the sun began to wane, more and more people filed into the inn, and it soon became too loud for him to make out one conversation from another. From what he could make out, all the talk was about the at-tacks of the bandits, who had hit many small farms around town a few weeks back, significantly raising the cost of food.

Thad decided he had heard enough. Everyone pointed out that the bandits cared little for the common person and used their venomous fangs on anyone who crossed their path. Wanting a bit of fresh air before he lay down for the night, he decided to take another stroll through the town.

As he walked into the poorer district of town, a ragged woman, who looked as if she hadn't taken a bath in her life, approached him. "Miss, would you happen to be interested in buying a young girl? She's healthy and a good worker." At first, Thad ignored the woman until she broke down and started crying. He turned back to lecture the woman about selling her own children, then he noticed a young girl about the age of seven, covered in as much dirt as the woman. She wore rags that barely covered her skinny underfed body. She tried to help the sobbing woman to her feet. Before he knew what he was doing, he went to the woman and began to help her to her feet, but instead, she grabbed hold of his leg, staring up at him with pleading eyes. "Please, I have another child still on the tit, and my husband was killed by the bandits not long ago. I don't have anything left to my name."

Thad always hated his mother for selling him into slavery, but she had already been well-off. This lady was just trying to save her other child, which he realized was held in the arms of the elder daughter. He went over to the little girl, holding his hands out to her for the baby. After a few seconds, she handed him the sleeping babe. The child was cute and looked well, but what surprised him was that the child was a boy. Most fam-ilies that fell on hard times would just drown a male baby.

The woman attached to his leg looked up at him. "Two gold." Her words shocked him. He had gone for over three thousand. "One gold, five silver," the woman countered, thinking his silence was an implied no. Thad handed the sleeping infant back to its mother, who, he noticed, took him lovingly, fear still etched in her face.

"Before I pay, I want to know—why not be rid of the male child?" He tried to make his voice harsh, and he figured he had done a fair job at it as the woman's face fell.

"He's just a babe, my baby," she said. The words were quiet as tears ran down her cheeks.

Thad dug into his coin pouch and counted out five gold coins and handed them to the lady. It took the woman a while to understand that he had paid well over what she was asking and thanked him through shocked tears. Not wanting to listen to the wailing sobs of the woman any longer, he motioned for the young child to follow him as he made his way back to the inn.

As soon as he was back at the inn, he walked up to the counter and asked for a bath and a second bed for the little girl as well as a small blind for some privacy. The innkeeper looked down at the dirty child and fla-shed him a big smile. "Anna has been trying to sell her to any well-off-looking person who passes through, but with the bandits about, no one was willing to take her on, even if she is a girl. Everyone in town has been helping out the ones the bandits devastated, but there's only so much we can do. The extra bed and bath are on the house. You just take good care of little Shariel there."

"I was wondering if there is a clothing shop still open. I don't want the girl to have to put on dirty clothes after the bath, and in all honesty, those clothes should be burned."

The innkeeper gave a little laugh. "Marel is the lady sitting over in the corner booth, the one wearing the light green dress with the matching bows in her hair. She owns the local tailor shop. Tell her what you want. Either she helps you, or I won't sell her another drink for a span."

Thad made his way over to Marel with Shariel silently following along at his heels. "The innkeeper said you would be the one to talk to about getting this girl some clean clothes so I don't have to smell these all night."

Marel looked at him, her face far from pleased until she noticed Shariel standing behind him. "I see Anna finally found someone to take her. It is such a sad situation. She truly loves her children." She turned to Shariel. "Let's get you some clothes, little one."

On the walk to the shop, Marel continued to chatter on. "You know, I offered to give Anna and her kids some clothes to help them out, but she refused any charity except food. If you don't mind me asking, I've seen little Shariel here grow up, and I'd like to know what you plan to do with her."

Her question caught him off guard, and he didn't have an answer for her until they reached the shop. He was glad the woman wasn't impatient or nagging, but he thought the woman deserved the truth, and for that, he needed to decide what he was going to do first.

Once inside the shop, Marel went straight to work, grabbing a tape measure and getting Shariel's sizes. "Honestly, I don't know what I'm going to do with the kid. At first, I wasn't going to buy her, but with the current state of her mother, I just couldn't let her stay in that situation. I can't even promise you the child will be safe as I travel a lot. All I can really tell you is that I'll do my best to make sure she is well taken care of."

"I guess that is about the best I could hope for. I wish you could promise me she would be safe, but with those bandits out there, killing everyone in sight, nowhere and no one is really safe," Marel said as she looked through her stocks for clothing of Shariel's size.

Thad ended up buying Shariel four dresses, three pairs of trousers, six blouses, two nightgowns, ten sets of undergarments, and two pairs of shoes. Marel tried to refuse full payment, but Thad insisted, telling her she could use the rest to help the next family.

Now that the child had a bigger wardrobe than him, they headed back to the inn, where the innkeeper informed him that the bed and bath were ready in his room. He asked that a couple of plates of food be sent up for them.

Once inside the comfort of the room, the little girl quickly shimmied out of her clothes and jumped in the tub, causing water to spill over the side, hitting the floor. Thad scolded her, but it wasn't very effective as he was laughing the whole time as he picked up a towel and began cleaning up the water. The girl was having trouble scrubbing off the massive amounts of dirt that had collected on her. Feeling slightly embarrassed about the situation, he picked up a rag and tried to help the girl by scrubbing her back. A young waitress brought the food to the door, and before she had a chance to leave, Thad roped her into helping get Shariel clean by promising her a silver coin.

Once the waitress had left and Shariel was clean, she finally looked human again. Her hair that had looked a dirty brown turned out to be a light blond. Her face was also adorned with freckles that made her look cute in a fierce way. Knowing he needed to explain some things to her, Thad brought her over to his bed and had her sit down. He could see her light blue eyes as they kept cutting over to the large plates of food waiting on the table. "We will eat in a second, but first, we have to talk about a few things. Have you ever heard of magic?"

The little girl's eyes lit up. "Yep, Papa used to tell me stories of mages who could call down lighting and make the whole sky light up," the girl said, throwing her hands up into the air.

"Now I want you to listen well. I am a mage." To accentuate his point, he called a small ball of light to his hand, gaining a gasp and happy clapping from the girl. "Now on this next part, I need you to stay calm. I'm not a woman. I'm a male."

The little girl stopped trying to grab at the light for a few seconds and gave him a quizzical stare. "You look like a girl to me."

Thad dispelled the light and illusion at the same time, earning another gasp from Shariel. "See? I'm a boy, but I dress as a girl when I'm around a lot of people. It's hard to explain why."

"Momma always said that some people treat men bad because they think they're bad people. Is that why?" the girl said shyly.

"That's close enough to the reason. So when I'm dressed like a girl, call me Clair. When I'm like this, call me Thad, OK?"

"OK, can we eat now?" Shariel said, looking hungrily at the food.

Thad chuckled. "Sure, let's eat."

The next day, Thad woke before the sun rose and pulled out two leftover cat's-eye gems and a few silver coins he had with him. After he had finished making two rings for Shariel, he donned his illusionary form and made his way to the common room of the inn. He paid for two plates of food to be sent up to his room.

When he returned to his room, Shariel ran to him, giving him a hard hug with tears in her eyes. "I thought you had left."

"Now, now. Calm down. I was just getting us some food. I also have a present for you, but you have to wait till after we eat to get it, OK?"

Shariel dug into the food as soon as it was sat down. She attacked the food in a warlike fashion. She finished well before Thad and almost seemed to dance in her seat, watching as he purposely ate as slow as pos-sible. Watching her dance about made it hard, but Thad did his best not to laugh. As soon as he finished his meal, he slowly made his way over to his travel sack, while Shariel danced around behind him, trying to see what he was getting from his bag.

After making sure both rings were securely hidden in his hand, he turned to Shariel. "Close your eyes." She almost glowed with anticipation as she squeezed her eyes so tight he was afraid she would strain something. Taking her hands, he slipped a ring onto the index finger of each hand.

As soon as the rings adjusted to her small fingers, she opened her eyes and squealed with delight. "They're so pretty."

"Not only that, but they're magical. The one on the left, if you say 'lumanare,' it will turn a light on and off, and the one on your right hand, if you say 'servo,' an invisible shield will protect you. Now I don't want you to play with the light in public, OK? The shield is only for emergencies. Don't use it unless you feel like you're in danger. Do you understand?"

"So no bad men can get me like they did Daddy?" She grabbed hold of him again and didn't let go. He could feel her shake as she softly cried, and the wetness from her tears soon soaked though his shirt. He didn't have any words for her, so he just hugged her back.

Before leaving town, Thad bought a nice palomino horse that Shariel named Spots. While he didn't mind walking, he couldn't bring himself to make Shariel walk all day long. After they were out of town, Shariel began asking where they were going. Thad knew he had to tell her but was afraid of how he should go about it.

"Listen, Shariel, we're headed to Avael, where the bad men who hurt your papa are. Once we're in town, I'm going to leave for a little while and punish the bad men, OK? When I leave, I'm going to give you a letter for a very good friend of mine, who will take care of you," Thad said, trying to keep his voice calm and reassuring.

"But the bad men might kill you. I don't want you to die," Shariel said sadly.

"They might, but if someone doesn't stop them, they will keep doing bad things. Plus do you think a few bad men can beat a mage? In any of the stories your daddy told you, did the mage ever lose?"

On foot, the trip to Avael would have taken four days, but on horseback, they arrived as the sun fell at the end of the second day. The trip was mostly uneventful, with few other travelers on the road. He and Shariel had plenty of time to talk. She was a smart girl and could read a little and do simple figures, but her education was lacking, something he decided would have to be rectified as soon as they got back to the capital.

Avael was a small logging community surrounded by a forest and had a large river running alongside the town, carrying logs to the various sawmills that were set up alongside it. While the town was small, the main street was bustling with activity as an armed militia patrolled the streets. Wanting to find information, he stopped the first armed group of men that he passed. They all wore dark leather uniforms and wore the Duchess of Calisaren's coat of arms.

"What is going on here?" Thad asked, making his voice as commanding as possible.

The four men snapped to attention. "My lady, a large group of bandits has been attacking travelers and landowners in the nearby area. We are here to protect this town until the royal army has been dispatched to deal with this threat."

News of the royal army made Thad's stomach tighten. "When do you expect the royal army to arrive?" Thad asked, trying to keep his voice level and calm.

"I don't know, my lady," the soldier replied, fidgeting slightly.

"That's distressing. Do you think you could point the way to an inn?"

The soldier relaxed slightly and pointed down the main road. "It's just a few blocks down, my lady."

Thad left the soldiers to their own affairs and continued down the road. He didn't like the idea of the royal army showing up. He had little doubt in his mind that if they showed up, they would try to place him in irons to be carted back to the queen. He didn't plan to let them, but they would try nonetheless.

The town inn wasn't fancy but looked clean. The inside of the inn had two common rooms, one for the males and one for females. Not wanting to waste time on idle banter, he made his way straight to the main counter, where an ancient-looking gentleman greeted him. "May I help you, my lady?"

"Yes, you may. I shall need a room with two beds as well as two baths and trays of your best food brought up. I will also need to see the proprietor of this inn when she is available."

The old man stuck his head through the door behind him, and a middle-aged woman with raven black hair, looking none too pleased to be disturbed, came marching out shortly after the man had disappeared. "What can I do for you?" Her voice carried as much displeasure as her face, with a fair bit of venom thrown in.

Thad handed her a letter addressed to Monique, along with three gold coins. Seeing the gold, her mood lightened considerably. "I must leave in the morning for a few days, and with the current bandit attacks, I do not wish to endanger my sister. I wish her to be well taken care of. If I should not return in a week's time, you are to get that letter to a Ms. Monique Torin. She is a merchant of the Rose Trading Company. She will see to the child and repay you for any expenses that my initial payment does not cover. Will that be acceptable?"

"Margret!" The woman yelled the name, and a young lady in her early twenties rushed up to the counter. "This little girl will be staying with us for a bit. I want you to introduce her to Melanie in the morning."

"Melanie is my granddaughter. They're about the same age, so they should get along well," she said, turning back to him.

After the long ride, hot bath, and warm food, Thad quickly fell asleep. He was awakened sometime in the night to Shariel screaming. His first reaction was showering the room in a bright light, thinking she was in danger, but as his eyes focused, he noticed her curled up in a fetal position, crying. He quickly went to her side. As soon as he sat down, she grabbed him around the waist tightly. He sat there, patting her back, until she fell asleep. After he was sure she was sound asleep, he tried to wiggle out of her grasp, but she was still holding on to him tightly. Afraid to wake her, he decided to give up on detaching the sleeping child and tried to get some sleep himself.

Thad awoke the next morning with his back and neck stiff from the awkward sleeping position. Shariel was still asleep, but she had rolled over sometime in the night, releasing him from her death grip. He quickly got dressed, and as he went to wake his young charge, a knock sounded at the door. He quickly donned his dis-guise and opened the door to find a wiry, bright-eyed, black-haired little girl. "Momma said I should come get your girl so we could go play." The girl rattled off, rocking back and forth and holding her hands behind her back.

"Well, I was just about to wake her up. If you'd like, you could do the honor for me."

A mischievous smile spread across the girl's face. Without another word, she advanced toward where Shariel was sleeping—like a wolf stalking her prey—then she pounced, landing right next to Shariel and bouncing her slightly in the air as she broke into a fit of bubbling laughter, which was quickly accompanied by Shariel's high-pitched laughter.

Shariel quickly got dressed and ran for the door with Melanie, but Thad pulled her up short. "One moment, Melanie. I need talk to Shariel for a moment," he said to the little girl, who pouted a little. "I promise she will be right down."

He turned back to Shariel and gave her a big smile. "Shariel, it is time for me to go hunt the bad guys. I have a bag of money here for you. Keep it hidden, and only use it if you have to. I promise I'll be back as quickly as I can. Until then, have fun, and play with your new friend." He pushed a bag of gold into her hand, and she quickly ran over to her bed and hid it within her pack. She then started to run out of the room but turned back before she reached the hallway and gave him a hug, then dashed out of sight.

CHAPTER VI

Thad walked with Spots, the palomino horse, trailing behind him as he searched the ground for signs of large groups of people entering or leaving the road. Before Thad left town, he had asked many of the soldiers for any recent news of the brigands and found that they were still in the area as they had been plaguing the road from Avael to Shiel using the forest to hide and move about unseen.

Thad was sure that if the brigands had set up camp in the area, they would have to have a central base of operations. If they stayed in the forest for cover, they would require campfires to cook and for warmth. While the smoke from a small fire would be hard to see thr-ough the trees, Thad suspected the number of people in the gang would require larger fires that were much harder to conceal.

As the sun began to set, he looked for a place off the road to make camp. Thankfully, all the main trade roads in the queendom had designated spots every five miles for people to camp, with a large pile of wood stacked for the use of campfires and a brick fireplace.

Sitting around the campfire, he stared at the trees. Since he was surrounded by forest, Thad couldn't see if there was any telltale smoke from a brigand's campfire. After walking up and down the road in each direction, he couldn't find a good vantage point to see over the canopy. Cursing his own stupidity, he made his way back to where he had camped.

When he got back to his camp, he found three men casually sitting at his fire, talking. As he approached, the men went silent, and one of the men raised his hand and greeted him. "Hello there, hope you don't mind us sharing your fire. When we first got here, we thought the bandits might have already gotten you. I'm Everit, shorty here is Isaac, and that mountain back there is Tack."

Thad examined the men closely; their clothes were well-worn. The man who had called to him was of average height and clean-shaven, with his long hair pulled back behind him. The man next to him reminded Thad of a rat with his disheveled short hair and days of patchy beard growth. He didn't have any visible wea-pons, but something about the way the man moved set his nerves on edge. The other man sat across from the fire. It was hard to tell much about the man as the fire pit and flickering flames mostly obscured him. His face was clearly visible, and his eyes followed Thad like a hunter's.

Thad put a smile on his face and raised his hand, greeting the men back. "I doubt the bandits would worry much about a lone traveler, let alone a man. I was just out trying to catch me some dinner—with little luck, I must say." He forced a smile to his face but kept his eyes trained on the men, watching them closely.

As he drew closer, the firelight caught the gems in his staff, and he noticed the rat-faced man smile and lick his lips. Unconsciously, Thad moved his hand to the hilt of his short sword and tightened the grip on his staff, his reaction getting a deadly laugh from the man who had greeted him. "I guess it's too much to ask to talk first?"

"We can talk, but if that little weasel comes near me, I'll skewer him," Thad said, mentally preparing his shield spell as he moved his hand away from his sword.

"I can see that you don't have an owner's mark, and you look as if you're doing well for yourself, but I doubt it has been easy. Me and some of my friends have gathered together to demand a change from the crown. Now I want you to think long and hard about your answer. I wouldn't want there to be a misunderstand-ding." While the men never moved for their weapons, Thad understood his meaning as he heard movement from the woods behind him.

"I have to admit, it hasn't been an easy life, and I agree that the current system could use a lot of work, but I won't give up my staff or my sword. I worked too hard to get them. So what do we do now?" Thad moved his hand back to his sword, crouching slightly as he eased his left foot out.

The rat-faced man dashed toward him as the man who Thad had figured to be this group's leader shouted for him to stop. The little man's movements were fast. His hand flashed almost magically, bringing two daggers to his hands. Thad had seen movements like that before. Assassins were always a fear of the peerage, and he had been trained long and hard on how to deal with them. When the man reached him, he lunged forward with both his daggers in one deft move. Thad swung his left leg back as his sword shot out of its sheath, severing the little man's head from his neck, then quickly reoriented himself on the two remaining men in the clearing as he let his invisible shield surround him.

The man behind the fire still hadn't moved, while the other man had his hand raised above his head. "Now that was unfortunate. Isaac was always a little excitable, but he had his uses. Why don't you put away your sword and come back with us to the camp?"

Thad weighed his options. If he fought, he was sure he could take out the two in the open, but he didn't know how many hid in the woods. While they didn't scare him, if any returned to their camp, they would be forewarned of his arrival. If he went with them, a number of things could go wrong, ranging from being poisoned to catching a knife while he slept. Bending down, he cleaned his blade on the fallen man's tunic and placed it back in its scabbard. At least this way, he would know where the bandits were. "No reason to waste any more time out here, is there?"

As soon as they were in the safety of the woods, they were joined by ten other men who, as Thad had expected, carried bows. Everit introduced them. Thad greeted each one, introducing himself as Mark. It felt odd to use his old name, but it was the only name that came to him besides using his own.

The moon was fully above them by the time they reached the outskirts of the camp. From the rumors he had heard, he had figured that he would face a ragtag band of at most fifty people. Surveying the massive amount of tents that littered the large clearing, it looked closer to a thousand. Thad let out a low whistle. "Quite a few more here than I expected."

Everit slapped him on the back. Thad knew he was a killer but just couldn't make himself hate the man. "Just pick a place to settle in for the night. I have to report the night's events, but I'll meet up with you in the morning and show you around."

Thad watched Everit as he made his way to the center of the camp and went into a large tent. With little else to do, Thad picketed Spots on the edge of the camp and laid out his bedroll. Wishing he had a spell to protect him while he slept, he clutched his staff tightly as he stared up at the star-filled sky.

The next morning, Everit met up with him a few hours after the sun had risen. The camp was larger than he thought, but there wasn't much to see. After a quick tour, they went to the mess area, where they were fed a tasteless gray gruel. Picking up a glob of the gruel and turning over his spoon, Thad watched it plop back into his wooden bowl with disgust. "So how do things work around here?"

Everit swallowed his mouthful of slop. "You get used to it." He chuckled, twirling his spoon in the air. "We have different groups that go out looking for supplies and new members or hitting the wealthy merchants' caravans. Most of the time, no more than a hundred men are gone from the main camp at a time. Our leader, Formir, collects information and gives us our assignments. It's a lot more organized than you would think."

"When did you join up with these guys?"

"I joined at the beginning. I was a dockworker in Shiphaven. Working all day, barely making enough to eat, and living in a group house when I met Formir. I was in a pub, complaining about the injustice of the world, drunk off my ass, when the pub owner took offense to something I said and had me whipped. Something inside me snapped, and I beat her to death before I knew what I was doing. Formir saw the whole thing and pulled me from the pub before the city guard could get me. That was over a year ago. We have been slowly gathering our strength and attacking where it will hurt the queen the most, taking her tax money. It hasn't been until recently that we have been able to make a bit of a dent, but soon, we can bring that bitch to her knees." Everit spoke passionately, but Thad wasn't convinced.

"I like the idea of making the laws more equal, but I have to admit that some of the things I've heard have me a bit worried." Thad knew that it was a risk to say such things, especially surrounded as he was, but if he just idly sat, it would take too long.

Everit gave him an understanding look. "I thought the same thing, but as Formir says, 'You need drastic measures to make drastic changes.' Formir is supposed to have some big news for us tonight. Before you make any rash decisions, why not hear what he has to say?"

"Sounds fair to me. What should I do until then?"

"Take a walk around, meet some of the other guys, and get to know them," Everit said, scraping the last of his food from his bowl.

Getting to know the others was the last thing he wanted to do. All it would do was make his job harder in the end. Many of these people just had a hard life, and their actions were a result of the faulted government system. While he could sympathize with the cause, he had to remind himself of those actions. If they had simply been targeting taxes or the peerage, he would join with them, but they made no distinction on whom they hurt as long as it furthered their goals. He was positive that if he had refused their offer the night before, they would have tried to kill him. If he allowed them to continue, Farlan would only be trading a neglectful regime for a cruel one. Either way, the current government was to blame for the current situation. While the laws didn't condone the current treatment of men, it didn't prohibit it either.

Farlan had been built around a simple idea. The Fae Wars had dragged on for over a hundred years after Emperor Tremon died. His heir had taken up his quest, and then his son after that. Emperor Tremon IV was young when he took the throne and, while not married, had many mistresses. When he was killed, many supposed heirs came forth, fighting over the imperial throne. A massive and bloody civil war followed, and the once-great empire collapsed. Lady Farlan, a countess, spoke of creating her own country on her land, where the crown would be passed down among the female line. While who had sown the seed could be questioned, no one could question who had given birth to it. With the civil war fresh in their minds, people flocked to Farlan, and the queendom was established. The queendom prospered, and after a few generations, all peerage titles were passed down among the female line. A few generations after that, all property was done so as well, and after that, men lost the ability to own property. What had begun as a brilliant idea had been taken too far and now threatened to cause the very civil war it had wanted to stop.

For a long time, Thad sat, staring at the ground, wondering what would be the best thing to do. Perhaps he could talk to this Formir and try to convince him into taking a better approach to the situation. He wouldn't know unless he tried. His mind heavy, he went back to his camp and brushed Spots down, trying to ease the uncomfortable knot that had formed in the pit of his stomach.

As the sun began to hang low on the horizon, a commotion stopped Thad's musings, and people began making their way to stand around the large tent in the middle of the camp. Thad followed the group, pushing his way as close to the front as he could.

Formir stood in the center of the commotion with two well-dressed men on each side. He was very tall and had a graceful build; his clothes were dignified, dyed a rich black and gray. His hooded brown eyes looked life-less, like two patches of dried blood. His thick straight obsidian hair was tied behind his head in a utilitarian style, giving Thad the overall impression of a snake.

Formir held up his hand, and the throng of men quieted. "My fellow revolutionaries, I have some bad news for you. The queen has ordered five hundred of her soldiers up from Southpass Fort to kill us." The men around him burst into shouts of anger and profanity. Formir waited for a bit, then signaled for them to silence again. "With our present number, we could most likely win, but at too heavy a cost. What we need is a more defensible base that will force them to take notice of us. If we can make our plight known, others will join us. Almost half of the queen's army is made up of slaves, and the rest are no better than slaves, living only off the queen's good graces. If given the chance, many of them will defect to our side." The crowd erupted into cheers. Formir waited a bit before quieting them down. "These two men are from the Kingdom of Abla, and they have pledged to help us in our plight. If we can force the queen to move enough of her troops from Southpass, then the Ablaian army will march, and together, we will force the queen to listen to our demands. To the south of here is Avael, where everything we need is available. Get some sleep, for tomorrow, we march, and by nightfall, Avael will be ours."

Thad's heart almost stopped in his chest. Avael? The bandits were going to attack Avael. As the speech wound down, people excitedly went back to their own camping areas, and soon, Thad was left alone with his thoughts. He watched as Formir and the two men from Alba went back into the large tent. The sun still stood above the edge of the trees, casting an orange glow over the tops of the foliage. He had to act quickly, before it got too dark out, or he would never survive the night, magic or no magic.

Looking around, everyone else was so busy celebrating that he doubted anyone would notice him. He still cast the glamour spell, and while it wasn't perfect, it would help keep people from focusing on him. Thad cautiously moved around to the back of the tent. Using his dagger, he cut a small slit and peeked into the tent. Formir and his two friends were sitting in fancy wooden chairs. Their voices were too soft to hear, so he cut a large-enough slit in the tent to crawl though. Once he was inside, he made his way over to the bed. Leaning against the headboard, he waited for his chance.

"Soon, the queen will have no choice but to weaken her army standing at Southpass, and we can take this country for our own," Formir said greedily.

"Yes, and the king will remember you fondly for your support in this, my lord," one of the Ablaian men said reassuringly.

"Remember the deal—you are to completely break the people here so that no one can rise up to challenge His Majesty. We do not want to have to deal with a rebellion. The kingdom cannot afford it," the other Ablaian said smugly. Thad could almost see the smirk on his face.

Thad cursed under his breath. It made perfect sense. Abla had been attacking Farlan every decade or so ever since they were founded. While they were also located by the ocean, their waterfront was littered with coral reefs, making it dangerous for ships to navigate, and inland, their soil was rocky and mountainous.

While they had one of the best sources of metal, everything else had to be brought in from the outside, and Farlan made a huge profit off their aggressive neighbors.

Not wanting to waste any more of the waning daylight, Thad went on the move, paralyzing all three of the men before stepping out of his concealment. His stomach tightened in knots as he moved toward the two men from Abla. The reckless group of misplaced revolutionaries was dangerous in its own right, but coupled with plots outside the queendom, it was even worse. Thad had to keep himself from vomiting as he cut the first man's throat. The second man's was easier, but it still felt wrong, killing someone as they simply sat there helplessly. He finally turned to Formir, whose eyes shook with fear. He placed the dagger to the man's throat. "I'm sorry, but I can't let you simply murder any more innocent people. If only you had gone about this a different way."

Thad went out the opening he had made in the back of the tent and moved back down to where Spots grazed. It only took a few moments to have the horse saddled and ready to ride, but he knew that the men around him would still most likely attack Avael in the morning, even with their leader dead. He had to slow them down, so he mounted Spots and raised his staff high above his head. Billowing balls of flame began to rain from the sky, consuming the main tent as well as anything else they touched. The stench of burned flesh filled his nose as the dying screams of hundreds of men reached his ears, causing his focus to waver and finally collapse as he leaned over the side of his horse to expel the contents of his stomach.

Wiping his mouth off with his sleeve, he noticed that people were pointing and yelling at him.

Figuring it was time to take his leave, he turned his horse about and galloped into the forest. As soon as he crossed into the woods, he felt a stabbing pain in his back. Instinctively, he reached behind himself with his right hand. Feeling a feathered shaft, he silently cursed himself for being too stupid to erect his shield.

He had to move slowly through the forest, and he dared not make his way onto the main road. His mind was starting to get fuzzy, and his hands started to shake. He knew he was losing too much blood; if he didn't make it to a healer soon, he wouldn't live to see the sun rise. His spirits rose slightly as the faint light from the town started to show through the trees. He was hurting too much to use his illusionary disguise, and he could only hope that the news he brought would be enough to secure him treatment.

He heard shouting and yelling as he made his way into town, and strong hands pulled him from his horse. He could hear voices, but he couldn't make out their meaning, but as strongly as he could, he kept repeating his warning. "Bandits coming in morning, thousands of them." He kept repeating the message over and over until his eyes rolled back into his head, and total blackness took him.

CHAPTER VII

The sky was still dark outside the window when he awoke, and pain stabbed through his body as he tried to sit up. A middle-aged woman gently pushed him back down. "You had a rough night, and you need to lie still for a bit. Move around too much, and you're going to rip the stitches in your back. You're lucky, you know. The arrow didn't go very deep, and I was able to get it out in one piece."

"You don't understand. The bandits are coming here. I killed their leader, but they're sure to still come," Thad said, gasping.

The woman gave him a concerned look. "Yes, you were mumbling about the bandits for quite some time. The guard has made preparations in case of attack. The town won't fall easily, so relax. Your sister has been frantic since we brought you in, but your other sister left a few days ago. Hopefully, she fares better on the road then you did."

The woman stepped out the door and called for Shariel. "Now, child, your brother is still sick, so don't be jumping on him, understood?"

Shariel nodded her head silently and walked over and sat beside his bed. Her eyes were puffy and swollen, and she looked as if she hadn't slept in days. He wanted to reassure her that he was OK, but the words wouldn't come to him, so he just placed his hand on her head. She instantly began crying again as she pulled his arm down, holding it tightly.

A knock on the door announced the presence of a sour-looking young woman in combat leathers, acc-ompanied by the innkeeper and Melanie. "Shariel, why don't you go play with Melanie a bit, and let your brother get some sleep. I promise you he's safe here."

Shariel didn't move until Melanie ran over to her and led her from the room by her arm. "Your sister cares deeply for you. She has been crying most the night," said the innkeeper, setting a pitcher of water on the table. "This is Captain Eloen. She wants to talk to you."

The innkeeper shut the door on her way out, leaving him alone with the young captain. The young lady had a beautiful and commanding figure, with her chestnut-colored hair that was cropped short and her narrow brown eyes, which resembled twin drops of chocolate. Her outfit hugged her body tight, showing off her luscious curves and soft cream-colored skin. "I am here for one thing—information. Why were you at the bandit camp? I need to know about their numbers, weapons, and training."

Thad painfully pushed himself up, then rearranged the pillows to allow him to sit up more comfortably. "Our parents were killed at their farm outside of Shiel. My sisters came here for safety, and I went after the bandits. I met up with them outside of town and killed one of them. Then I was given the choice to either go with them or be left dead on the road, so I went with them. Once at their camp, the sheer number of them shocked me. There was around a tho-usand, all led by one man. I don't have an answer for you about weapons and training. I was only there a short time. Last night, the leader gave a speech outlining his plan to attack this town. For fear for my sisters, I snuck into his tent and killed him, then set fire to the tents and ran. I took an arrow as I was leaving, and the rest, you know."

"We saw a large amount of smoke from the forest. We had thought the bandits had raided another caravan. It is nice to hear it was their bodies burning for once. The amount is quite a bit more than we thought. Are you sure it was a thousand? From what we have gathered, there should only be about one hundred." Her voice, while calm, carried a condescending tone.

His patience was quickly wearing thin. "Listen, I'm not some dullard that can't count past the number of fingers and toes he has. If you put my family in danger because you're too self-important to listen to a man, you won't have to worry about what the bandits will do to you because I'll kill you before they can get to you."

Eloen reached down and grabbed his nightshirt and pulled him toward her, then gave him a rough kiss. Her lips were soft, and she smelled of leather and vanilla. "Don't you worry. We're already putting up a makeshift wall with the logs, and everyone in town is working. If they attack, they may overrun us, but they won't do it easily." Eloen trailed her hand up to his cheek, then, giving it a light slap, she smiled and left him alone with his thoughts.

The day passed quickly while Thad drifted in and out of sleep. Shariel brought his meals to him but never said anything to him. Her face shifted constantly between a sad and betrayed look. He could understand it somewhat. He had promised her he would be all right but had ridden back into town near death. Though they had only known each other for a short time, Shariel had lost everything and was looking for anything to hold on to, to keep from drowning in her own sorrow.

After sleeping throughout most of the day, he had trouble sleeping that night. He would be tired tomorrow, but there was little he could do about it now. Shariel had crawled into bed with him and had curled up against his side; it had taken a while for her to fall asleep, and even then, she seemed to be fitful. Every now and then, she shifted, sending a slight jolt of pain coursing though his back, but he didn't have the heart to make her move.

The noise started shortly after the sun began to peek through the windows in his room. Twisting painfully, he looked out to see the militia running around and forming defensive ranks along the newly constructed barricades. There could have been no more than two hundred or so soldiers to the bandits' thousand. Knowing that the defenders couldn't last long without help, he shook Shariel awake. "Shariel, the bad guys are here. I want you to go hide. Do you remember how to use your rings?" She nodded her head as tears welled up in her eyes.

Thad strapped on his sword and slowly made his way down the stairs using his staff to hold himself up. By the time he made his way outside, it looked as if the defenders were already being overcome on the northern side. He needed a better vantage point in order to be effective. Looking around, he noticed Eloen standing on a raised platform near the middle of the town, yelling out orders to the soldiers, a host of archers surrounding her, putting their deadly bows to work.

He quickly hobbled over to where she stood and began climbing the ladder. Each rail seemed to hurt more than the last, but he pushed on. As he reached the top, Eloen, who must have been told of his approach, helped pull him to his feet. "What in the nine hells are you doing out here? I should kick your ass and send you back, but with the way things look, I wouldn't turn away an armed man right now."

"Just watch, and keep them off me the best you can." She gave him a questioning look, but he didn't have time to explain himself. Pointing his staff in front of him, he focused his energies and sent a blast of lighting out at the most densely packed group of attackers. He heard the people around him gasp but didn't have time to worry about their reaction. He sent blast after blast of lighting. At one point, the eastern wall was almost breached, so he made a wall of flame, forcing the attackers to move back as arrows peppered them. After his initial assault, many of the bandits had turned and ran, while others had approached more cautiously, giving the defenders more time to reposition and repel the attacks. Soon, the bandits were losing all heart for the battle, but Thad dared not let up. He had to make sure Shariel was safe.

Suddenly, everything was moving. The ground rushed up to him as his legs gave out, and he fell forward toward the ground below him. Pain ripped through his back as someone grabbed him from behind, slamming him hard onto the wood. He tried to stand, but his body wouldn't heed his command. His last vision was that of Eloen's lips pressing softly against his own.

Thad awoke with his head pounding, as if an army of blacksmiths were using it as an anvil. A small strand of light invading through the closed shutters flickered across his face. It was like a red-hot poker to his mind. Sitting up, a wave of nausea rolled over him. He set his hand down to steady himself, and it landed on something soft and warm. Following his eyes to what his hand had found, all the blood rushed to his face as he realized it rested on a naked breast. He quickly brought his offending hand back to his own chest and then rubbed his eyes, willing them to focus. He was rewarded with Eloen's smiling face staring up at him.

"I was wondering how long you were going to sleep," Eloen said, sitting up, the light sheet falling away. Her breasts were small and perky, with small light pink nipples. Thad couldn't help but let his eyes slowly lower to her hard stomach and then to the light hazelnut hair that peeked out from the top of the covers. He strained his eyes, his head pounding more, trying to will the sheet to fall just a little more. Suddenly, he was brought back to his senses as Eloen let out a light giggle.

Thad's face turned a bright red as he noticed that the sight of her naked body had gotten more than a small reaction from his body. Placing his hands over the offending body part, he stuttered an apology.

Seeming to enjoy his discomfort, Eloen ran one of her fingers up his chest. "You're so innocent. It's cute." As her finger reached the underside of his chin, she leaned in, giving him a warm kiss, her tongue darting in his mouth. At first, it felt odd, but he soon found his body responding without thought. His hands moved up her back, pulling her into a deeper kiss. After a few seconds, she pushed him back, giving him a sultry smile. "As much as I would like to show you the pleasures of a woman, we need to talk. Now that the threat to the area is more or less gone and the royal army will be here shortly to round up the rest of the vagabonds, I will be required to report to my duchess what transpired here. I am fully aware that without your help, the town would have been lost, but I also know there aren't a lot of mages running around. Your antics at the palace, and the fact that the queen wants you in the worst way, are common knowledge."

As she spoke, Thad slowly scooted to the edge of the bed, all thoughts of the kiss gone from his mind as he tried to figure out how to escape. Before he could stand, he was suddenly stopped by Eloen's strong hand. "Don't worry, I'm not going to arrest you, and even if I did, I know nothing of mages, and after seeing what you're capable of, I don't fancy being burned to a crisp. No, what I was going to say is that you need to be gone before the army gets here. As grateful as everyone is, someone is still bound to tell them who you are." She smiled teasingly, running her hand over his cheek. "Now that all the boring stuff is out of the way, we could continue where we left off." Her words trailed off as her hands pulled him into another kiss, but their fun was short-lived as the door to his room burst open.

He pulled the sheet up, covering his chest, as a very mad-looking Monique stomped over to him. "What in the nine levels of the abyss?" The look she leveled him made him want to jump out the nearest window because no matter how painful dying might be, he dou-bted it had anything on what she could inflict. "I get into town and hear of a mage who fought off a throng of attacking bandits only to collapse at the end of the battle and stay unconscious for days, so I rush up here to check on you, and what do I find but you fooling around with some jezebel!"

"There's nothing wrong with some harmless fun. Maybe if you tried it, you wouldn't be wound so tight," Eloen said, getting up from the bed, unabashed by her nude form, and began putting on her battle leathers. "Next time we meet, Thaddeus, we will have to pick up where we left off." She gave a slight giggle as his face turned bright red and left him alone with a steaming Monique.

"She was here when I woke up … I didn't … well, you see …" Thad placed his hands over his face as his headache seemed to strike back with full force.

Monique crossed her arms over her chest while looking down at him, her eyes like daggers. "So you're telling me you weren't in here, running your hands all over her body, while you tried to see how much of your tongue you could cram in her mouth."

Thad hung his head. What could he say that wasn't an obvious lie? "I'm sorry."

Monique dropped down hard on his bed, took a few deep breaths, and let a smile show on her face, though it didn't seem to reach her eyes. "Why don't you tell me what you've been up to? When I arrived and came to inquire about you, the innkeeper gave me your message, and I must admit, it gave me a bit of a shock, so I might have overreacted a little."

Thad relayed everything that had happened to him since they had last parted. Monique laughed and gasped at the appropriate parts of the story and grabbed his hand, giving it a tight squeeze, when he got to the part about Shariel.

"Sounds like you've had quite the adventure, and you say you've been dressing as a female? I would love to see that," she said, giggling slightly. "A meeting with the queen—that's great, though I'm going to have to think of a way to deflect her questions away from the magical items. What do you plan to do with the kid? I don't think a sewer is a good place to raise her."

"I want to get her into the school in the capital. I was thinking about tagging along with you to your meeting with the queen and petitioning her for the right to buy a house and allowing Shariel to attend the school. I can always sell my magical items for money. Though as I promised, the majority will still be going to you. On that matter, I have a lot of them ready for you back in the capital."

Monique rubbed her chin. She always did that when she was thinking. Thad found it slightly on the adorable side. "Seems like a good plan. If it doesn't work, well, we can just worry about that then. Now if I understand the situation right, we need to get you out of town quickly and quietly. I think the innkeeper is the only one who knows I'm connected to you. I'll talk to her, and tonight, we will sneak you and Shariel into the coach."

Monique was nice enough to step outside and let him get dressed, though she did tease him about his sudden shyness. When Shariel showed up with their meals, Monique's attitude changed completely as she began fawning over the little girl. Thad had to fight to keep from laughing at the two of them. When he became the subject of the conversation, though, his face quickly turned bright red as the two girls made him seem like the kid who was in need of a caregiver.

After night had fully fallen, he and Shariel were visited by Brand, who, with the help of the innkeeper, snuck them out of the back door and into the waiting coach. They wouldn't leave right away, but later the next day so as to leave the impression that he and his young charge had disappeared in the middle of the night. It was a great plan and one that Monique was very proud of.

Thad let Shariel take the bed as he lay down to sleep on the hard floor. His body was still sore, and his stitches pulled at his back every time he moved to try and find a more comfortable position, but it still didn't take him long to fall asleep. His mind was still exhausted from the battle.

The next morning started out well, but as the noise of kids merrily playing outside reached Shariel's ears, it became increasingly difficult to keep her quiet. When Monique finally stepped inside the coach and informed them of their impending departure, he could have almost jumped for joy. While he had little knowledge of how to keep a seven-year-old girl entertained, Monique seemed to excel at it. In no time, Monique was braiding Shariel's long blond hair, wrapping the dual ponytails with strips of bright green ribbon. She then let Shariel go through her jewelry box and try everything on. With each new piece, she would grab a little hand mirror and inspect to see how it looked. At one point, she had so many pieces adorning her that Thad couldn't help but laugh, though he regretted his decision as soon as both girls turned on him. "What, don't I look pretty?"

She had a ring on each finger, four necklaces, and a pair of small pearl stud earrings, her ears still red where Monique had pierced them, and to top it off, she had on one of Monique's dark silk dresses that seemed to swallow her. "Yes, you do. I would say any prince would beg you for a kiss." Shariel gave a high-pitched squeal, rushing over and giving him a peck on the cheek, gaining a laugh from Monique. All of a sudden, the idea of living in the palace dungeons didn't seem like such a bad idea.

Traveling with a caravan was slow, and for the first two days, Monique refused to let him out of the coach except for short stops. He tried arguing that the army wouldn't make it this far yet, but she refused to allow him free reign until his magic had recuperated to the point where he could safely use it. When he woke on the third day, the pressure in his head had completely disappeared, so he cast a small light spell. When he got no immediate pain from the feedback, he tried his disguise.

He could almost cry out in happiness but refrained so as to not wake the two girls still sleeping on the bed. Spending every waking moment with a young lady might seem fun, but Monique spent most of her time showing Shariel how to do beadwork to pass the time, leaving him with nothing to do. Most the time, when he tried to strike up a conversation, she hushed him. He might have thought that after all his time alone in the sewers, he would have been used to being alone, but without his books and magic to keep him company, he was going stir-crazy.

He could have snuck out while Monique was sleeping, but he feared how she would respond if she woke with him gone. Looking down at the two sleeping forms, he wondered if they were anything like a real family. Monique sat up, stretching her arms wide and letting out something between a yawn and a groan. "Feeling better today?" she said, rubbing the sleep from her eyes.

As was their morning ritual, Thad turned around as Monique roused Shariel from her slumber, usually by tickling the poor child until she was close to tears. "Yes, the headache is finally gone, and I already tested my magic. It seems I'm completely healthy again." He could hear Monique getting dressed, and he had to fight the urge to peek over his shoulder. She had warned him that if he did, they would be giving the horses a break, and he would be pulling one of the carriages for the day. He was not altogether sure if she was joking.

"We should be reaching Shiel sometime this afternoon, and since we have to keep up the facade that you're a woman, you will have to have your own room. Shariel can sleep in a room with me. Do you need anything from town? I need to see if I can sell some of the wool and meats I picked up in Tremon. I heard about the attacks on the farms while I was down there, and I figured I could make a hefty profit." Thad gave her a sad look. "Don't give me that. We're merchants. I understand people are hurting, but I'm not running a charity. Don't worry, I won't charge them too much. Just enough to make a fair profit."

Thad understood what she was saying, but it just didn't feel right for him to charge any more than nece-ssary when people were in need. That might have something to do with his upbringing. The academy not only prided itself in making the best slaves but in making ones with a good moral center. They were forced to read histories of what the worst of men could do with great power and of what the best of men could with little.

As soon as they got to town, Monique and Shariel disappeared, leaving him alone for the first time in days. Wearing his disguise, he found Brand along with a few of the other guards sitting in the common room of the inn, drinking. As soon as Brand had learned of his disguise, he hadn't wasted any time in teasing Thad. Before he had the chance to take a seat, Brand jumped from his chair and made a lavish show of helping him sit. "My lady, to what do we owe this glorious honor?" Brand said, bowing at the waist. Thad could see the smile twitching at the corners of Brand's mouth.

After a few ales, a lot of laughs, and more than a few jokes at his expense, he went back up to his room and kicked back on his bed. Though his magic power was slowly increasing, he had to find a better way to fight. The battle back at Avael proved that. His rune necklace worked well but still had its limits. He would have to link hundreds of gems for what he wanted, but there was no way he could wear that many. If there was a way for him to access the power remotely, it could be done, but how? If it had a massive core, it could work, but where would he find something large enough?

His thinking was shattered as Shariel ran into the room, twirling around in a new dark blue dress, with Monique following behind her. "Do you like it, Thad? Monique got it for me, and look," she said, pulling back her hair to show off two small earrings.

"You look beautiful," he said as she twirled around the room.

"Monique bought me a lot of new dresses. Wanna see them?" Shariel said, rushing over to poor Collin, who stumbled into the room laden down with packages. For the next few hours, he was tortured into watching as Shariel changed from outfit to outfit, showing off her new wardrobe.

The next day, as they continued their journey to the capital, Shariel rode with Collin at the front of the coach, while Thad and Monique discussed what they were going to do once they reached their destination. "First thing, we will have to get an audience with the queen. We can send Shariel with a letter of our interest for a visit. With what you have said, they shouldn't let us wait for more than a day or two. Have you decided how to get the initial money for the house and tuition for school?"

"No, I just figured I could sell some of my items for the needed coin, though honestly, I have no idea how much a house will cost in the capital," Thad said softly.

"It depends on how big of a house you want and what part of the city you want to live in. I would suggest a three-bedroom in the nice district. It would cost you around four hundred gold. I don't know how much tu-ition for the school is, but I doubt it will be over twenty gold coins a year."

Thad's eyes widened in surprise. Four hundred gold was a lot more than he figured. "Unless I sell most of the stock I have made for you, I don't think I can come anywhere near that. I might have to find a place to rent for the time being."

"You could do that, but I would suggest that you borrow the money from a lender. You will have to make a scheduled payment, and I can write you a writ of par-tnership, which should allow you to borrow what you need. That is, if the queen allows it since you will be petitioning to purchase as a noncitizen. I would also suggest you put the house in Shariel's name just in case."

Over the next two days, they went over everything from how they would dress to what they would say to the queen. As far as the magical items went, they would try and skip over the details, only saying that they had met up with a contact that had agreed to allow them to sell the items. It wasn't a perfect plan, but unless Thad wanted to expose himself, it was the best they could do.

When they reached the city, Monique acquired them rooms at the Double Dove Inn, while he made his way down to his sewer lair and collected the bags of magical items he had prepared for her. The bags were heavy and filled with items such as simple glowing candlesticks, rings that kept you dry in the rain, knives that would cut through steel, and his favorite, a magical wand that cleaned clothes.

Once back at the inn and secure in Monique's room, he laid out everything and began explaining them to her. "I made about fifty of the light rings, forty magic blades, eighteen magical boxes, each with two command codes. The individual ones are inside the boxes, while the master code is your name. Those are all my earlier work with crystals and some cheap gems I came across later that are extremely well suited to magic and much stronger."

Monique picked up one of the new rings and examined it closely. "A cat's-eye gem. I never understood why people don't use them more often. I think they're beautiful."

"Yes, cat's-eye gems are cheap compared to anything else that matches them in magical potential. With those, I made around thirty magical candlesticks, a few magical boxes that light up when opened, a dozen more shield rings, fifty magical cleaning wands, and a host of other smaller things you had me make for you last time. Here is a list of everything and how they work," he said, handing her a handful of butcher paper with charcoal writing.

Monique shook her head, laughing slightly. "Ser-iously, you have to get some proper writing materials, but I must say, this is much more than I thought you wo-uld have ready for me. At the rate you can make these, I wish I could send another caravan as soon as I get back to Rane, but I would have to hire more people."

She gave him a soft kiss on his cheek and placed a small bag of gold into his hand. "Here, I wish I could give you more, but I just can't right now. Next time I see you, though, I should have enough to keep you well enough for some time."

As soon as the sun rose the next day, they sent Shariel to the palace with their introduction letter. It took three days for them to hear back. They were invited to dine with Her Majesty for supper. Though Monique had warned him of the delay, she still didn't seem to enjoy wasting time from the road. While they waited, she sold some of his magical items and procured some other goods to sell on her way back north.

Shariel begged to come along with them to the castle, and after over an hour of telling her no, she finally stalked off to her room to pout. Watching her cry made him feel bad, but they had no idea what the queen would say, and he didn't want to give the poor kid any false hope.

They were greeted at the palace gate by Kris, the friendly older gentleman who had been his companion the first few days outside the academy. Thad was glad he looked well. He had often wondered about what had happened to the old man after the attack. The old man looked over their gift, which was just one of his shield rings with a cat's-eye gem, then led them to a small dining hall, which, while richly decorated, didn't flaunt wealth like the one he had eaten in during his previous visit to the palace.

He had expected there to be a large group of people attending but was astounded to find that it was just him, Monique, Maria, and the queen. They presented their gift to the queen, who graciously took it, then handed it to one of her attendants.

"Let's enjoy the meal first, and then we can talk business. I believe that is the custom in Rane, is it not?" the queen said, motioning to the table.

The meal was simple but served on the most elegant dinnerware he had ever seen. They talked of simple things, but when the news of the battle at Avael was brought up, the queen suddenly took a great interest. "So you were there for the battle? Is it true that a male mage fought them back single-handedly?"

"No, Your Majesty, we arrived a few days after the battle, but that was the general story around town. A male arrived, wounded by an arrow, and he told the town guards of the vast horde of men coming. From what I heard, he killed the bandits' leader before making his way to the town. When they attacked, the militia was hard-pressed, and defeat was certain, then the man emerged from his bed and rained down fire and lighting, forcing the bandits to retreat." Monique did a good job of telling the story, emphasizing all the exciting parts.

Thad noticed that Maria was staring daggers at Monique and him the whole time; he wasn't sure what it was about but wished he could have a few moments alone with her to find out.

As soon as the meal was cleared away, the queen wasted no time and launched right into the discussion. "It has come to my knowledge that your company has come into a vast quantity of magical items. What I really want to know is where they're coming from."

"Your Majesty, all I can say is that we have a deal with an individual for the sole rights to the sale of the magical artifacts he has. If I say more than that, I might as well cut my own throat." Thad had learned from Monique that the saying "cut my own throat" was a polite way of saying that it was a protected subject.

The queen gave a slight frown but quickly recovered, resealing her emotions behind an impassive face. "I feared that would be the case. May I ask if I can make an order for specific magical items, or is there only a limited selection of items?"

"We have had mixed success with requesting specific magical items, but my source has been known to procure most anything we have asked them to acquire."

"Well, while having magical lights or these eme-rgency shields would be handy, I was thinking more along the lines of swords. I have heard tales of magical swords so sharp they could cut through metal. Do you think an order of one hundred at a cost of, let's say, fifteen gold apiece would be agreeable?"

"I can't give you an answer right now, but as long as my source is able to procure the items, I believe we could have them ready for you in, let's say, two months' time. To help facilitate our business, I would be willing to leave Clair here to help," Monique replied after a few moments of thought.

The queen's eyes widened considerably. "Two months? Is the Rane calendar different from our own? I didn't know you could reach Rane and return within a span of sixty-four days."

Thad's mind began reeling as their story fell apart, but Monique never seemed to miss a step. "You're right, Your Majesty. It would be impossible by normal means, but our source has given me items so that I may communicate with him and transfer goods over long distances. I apologize to Your Majesty, but we are enc-roaching on protected territory again. I have already said more than I should have."

"Well, I think leaving Clair in town, readily av-ailable, would be a great idea. I believe she and my daughter have already struck up a friendship."

"There is just one problem, Your Majesty. Clair has a younger sister who is traveling with her due to the tragic loss of their father. They would need permission to purchase a house. Also I think Clair would like to get her sister into school in the near future."

"That can be arranged. I will send a letter to the proper channels, so you need not worry on that end, but the new term will not start until after the first of the year. I would advise you visit with the school administrator."

Shariel was excited when they told her that she would be living and going to school in the capital. They allowed her to go with them when they went to the housing authority. They looked at a lot of houses and finally decided on a three-bedroom house near the market district. Thanks to the queen, the price wasn't extravagant and was set at a low 350 gold. After a stop at the local lenders' guild, they got a loan for the money to be paid back over five years at only seven gold pieces a month. With thirteen months a year, it added up to over a hundred gold in interest, but Monique told him it was a fair rate for such a large unsecured loan.

Chapter VIII

The school administrator was an older woman, easily in her late fifties, with dark brown hair with traces of light silver shining through. She was slightly plump with a bright, almost-radiant smile. "Ms. Torin, as you are already aware, the term for this year has already started, but if you are truly serious about your sister attending here, I would suggest a tutorship with one of our older students. Now while most would believe we only cater to the rich, we have a fair amount of children who attend here on scholarship from the queen who would be more than willing to help your sister catch up on her studies. If that sounds acceptable, then have her here before first bell in the morning. Now as for tuition, it is ten gold a year. That includes food. If she requires lodging, it will be an additional five gold. As for the tutoring for the rest of the term, I believe four gold will more than cover the cost."

After a quick stop by the school's accountant, he made his way back home, where Shariel was making lunch. Though still young, she was handy around the house. He guessed it was one of the benefits of having grown up on a small farm where everyone was forced to do their part; thinking back, Joan's farm worked much the same way.

As they ate, Thad told Shariel of the tutoring she was to receive starting the next morning. When she found out that the school would take up most of her day, she was none too pleased. "Now listen. You're there to study, and right now, you're pretty far behind in your schooling. You will have to go six days of the week, but that still leaves you three days of your own.

If you work hard, I'll even give you a silver each week, which you can spend on anything you want."

Shariel completely forgot about school and began talking about what she would get with her first allowance. After the meal, he decided to head down to the local blacksmith to see about some swords. Shariel tagged along as far as the first trinket stand. Smiling, he told her to be home by supper and continued on to the blacksmith's.

The inside of the shop was clean, and after a quick talk with the lady running the shop, a bald six-foot giant of a man wearing a thick leather apron came into the room.

"Margret tells me you have a specific request."

"Yes, I need an order of one hundred long swords. I need them made fast and cheap. I don't need them to hold an edge long, but I do need them to be well balanced, and I don't want plain hilts on them either. I would like something pleasing to the eye."

The man scratched his chin. "If I made a molding, I could put them out fairly quickly. It would still take about three weeks to get them all done, but they won't be as strong as forged steel, and as you said, they won't hold an edge long. Would that be acceptable?"

"That would be perfect. How much to have all one hundred made as quickly as possible?"

"Well, first, we will have to make the first sword and hilt, then the moldings for a hundred swords. We will need about four molds. After that, my apprentice can do most of the work. I would suggest to Margret a sum of around 120 gold."

He had brought all his gold with him, but even with everything Monique had left him, he only had a little over eighty gold, and if he wanted any more gold, he was going to have to buy materials in order to make more magical products. "I will give you half down and will pay the rest when the first quarter of the product is delivered. If you can turn them out as fast as you say and they are what I need, then I would suspect making more orders in the future."

The woman behind the counter, who had stayed silent during the discussion, had a big smile. "That would be fine, miss. Now why don't we let Bruno get back to work while we settle accounts?" Thad counted out the gold to the greedy-eyed lady, who practically salivated over the gold, then gave her directions to his home for the delivery.

After buying enchantment supplies, food, and a few other household items, his gold pouch was near empty. If he wanted to make his house payment and get the gold for his order of swords, he was going to have to work very hard. After a quick stop at his house, Thad made his way to the familiar sewer entrance in the squatter's district.

The next few weeks passed by in a uniform manner with Shariel headed to school and him to the sewer to work. He had already made a fair amount of items, half of which he sat aside for Monique. He had made nearly forty gold, but the deadline for his payment to the blacksmith was closing in fast.

Rubbing his head from the stress of the day's work, he made his way back to his house. Inside the house, he was greeted by Shariel, who introduced him to a young lady in her early twenties with round chocolate-colored eyes and silky, straight, medium-length charc-oal-colored hair that she wore in an exotic, yet attractive style. "Clair, this is Willow. She is one of the senior students at the school. She heard that you had contacts with a magical dealer and wished to talk to you." Shariel hedged about looking guilty. She wasn't telling the whole truth, but he saw no harm in the current situation.

Straightening his dress, he sent Shariel to grab them some tea. "I guess asking how you found out I have contacts with items of magical significance is moot. It's no secret that our company has been selling them. As for where I live, I can take a guess as to how you found out, but the main question here is what do you need?"

Willow didn't strike him as the type to mince words, and with his head aching, he was glad he was right. "I am in need of a book that will allow me to carry a variable library around with me. This is my last year at school, and there are quite a few tomes I wish to have copies of. While I could hire someone at the scribes' guild to copy them, toting so many books back home would prove troublesome."

A book that could hold more than one book within it—he hadn't thought of that before. While paper was made of wood, it was too thin and weak to hold an enchantment, and then there was the problem of copying the books, then calling the book you wanted. If he was to use a central core along with a thin metal layer over the cover, it could work, but how would he get it to copy? What if he put a second gem and enchantment on the back of the book? With that, it should be possible. "I am sure I could acquire something of that nature in a few weeks' time, but it wouldn't be cheap. You're not asking for some run-of-the-mill artifact, but one that would have been prized even among the mages of the past."

"Well, if I was to have each of the books I wanted copied, it would cost me around eight gold. For a magical book, I would be willing to pay twenty."

"I'm sorry, but that wouldn't be enough. We're not talking about a simple item here, but a magical book that can copy any book quickly to be recalled later at any time. For that, I would have to demand forty gold." After a bit of haggling back and forth, the pick was decided on thirty-two gold with half up front—that being Willow's request—most likely to make him work harder to get her product. It was much harder to tell someone you couldn't get his or her order when you had already received payment.

After Willow had left, Thad went straight to the local scribe store and got three thick blank books as well as ten smaller ones for the initial experimentation. The idea of a magical book intrigued him; if it worked, he could have Shariel use it to copy some of the books from the school's library for him to read at his leisure. Mak-ing the cover with steel didn't seem right, so he splurged on a bar of silver.

Over the next few days, he spent most of his time working on the magical tome. It seemed like an easy-enough idea, just make it copy the book, but it was a lot more complicated than he thought. After a few trials and errors using the smaller books, he found that all he needed to do was to have the tome copy anything within a designated area. After that, he just had to set the perimeters. After the book was copied, gold flowing script would appear on the front of the tome that when touched and read would force the book to recall the selected item. Before he could give Willow her copy, he had to see just how many books it could hold. So that night, he passed the book to Shariel for instruction on how to make it work as well as what kinds of books he wanted copied.

The day seemed to drag on as he waited for Shariel to come back from the school. He tried to keep himself busy, playing around with a few new rings, but couldn't hold his focus due to the anticipation. When she finally returned home, she gave him a sad, put-upon look. "My tutor saw me with the history books and thought I liked them. I had to spend all day reading." The disgust in her voice matched with the vision he got of her sifting through a mountain of books and made him laugh.

The tome had done much better than he had figured and had been able to store a total of forty-six books. Flipping through one of the books he had been waiting to read, he gave Shariel a big hug. He dug into his coin pouch, pulled out a single gold, and tossed it to her. "For testing it for me." Shariel caught the coin deftly and began jumping around the room.

As word started getting around that he could get magical artifacts, he found himself beleaguered by people wishing to have things made, from the mundane to the impossible. To solve his problem, he started telling everyone to simply send him a description of what they were looking for, and if he could procure their order, he would be in contact. While the constant interr-uptions were annoying, they did allow him to make a large sum of gold, which brought along an idea of his own. Monique had lied to the queen that he had a way for them to communicate and deliver items over long distances. What if he really could make such an item? She could take specific orders, and he could send them to her.

A couple of days into the work for what he called the sending box, the first order of swords was delivered. He was now in possession of large amounts of gold, so paying the remainder for the swords was quite easy. He had a fair amount of anticipation when he ope-ned the crate, wondering what design Bruno had come up with for the hilts. The blade was simple as he exp-ected, but the guard looked like two talons stretching out from a scaled hilt.

As he began working on the swords, the princess made her way to visit him at his sewer home. He had thought she would have come to visit much sooner and had even entertained the idea to go visit her, but he didn't want to push his luck. One wrong step within the palace and he would find himself in prison.

The princess watched him closely as he worked on the swords her mother had requested. Setting down the sword he had just finished, he turned to the princess. "I figured that you would have come to visit me sooner. I've missed your banter."

"I didn't want to interrupt your time with your new friend." While the princess's face stayed impassive, her voice showed more than a hint of irritation. He knew she was mad. He just wasn't sure about what. Maybe he should have visited her sooner.

"Monique? She left the day after our audience with the queen. I've told you about her. She is like my sister. I'm sorry I haven't visited the palace, but with everything going on, I just haven't had the chance, not to mention I'm still a little worried about spending time around the palace."

Maria gave him a harsh stare for a bit, then a smile slowly crept onto her face, and she rushed over to him, embracing him in a tight hug. "So tell me everyt-hing that happened. The stories we've been getting are garbled by the distance, and I have no idea what actually happened in Shiel."

Thad relayed the story, telling her of how he had purchased Shariel from a woman who had been attacked by the bandits. Maria was quite interested in his new charge, asking every question from her age to what her hobbies were. After her curiosity about Shariel was sated, he continued with the story. When he got to the part about the Ablaian spies, she looked worried and fussed over him profusely when he got to the part where he took an arrow in the back. Her attitude changed from concerned to outraged as he related his meeting with Eloen.

"So the Ablaians are riling up the males in order to weaken us so they can attack. This isn't good, and I can't tell Mother, or she will wonder where I learned it from. Unfortunately, our plan didn't work as I hoped. Mother is looking for you even harder now."

Thad looked at the princess in a new light. Though he had talked with her often, it dawned on him that she acted much older than her age. An eleven-year-old should be playing and having fun, not talking to a mage in a musky sewer. "Are you sure you're eleven?" The words popped out of his mouth before he had a chance to think better about it. He looked at the princess for any sign of anger, but she just gave him a glowing smile.

"I was wondering how long it would take you to notice. Since I was three years old, I have been groomed to be the next queen. Every day, I'm reminded that everything I say and do affect the queendom."

Maria's face fell slightly, and Thad could see she mourned her lost childhood. He himself had been trained since early childhood to be perfect, but the mothers at the academy had insisted that they enjoy some time to be kids. He had asked one time and was told that being serious all the time is bad for one's heart. "I don't think the Ablaians will give up on just one attempt. As soon as I have a chance, I will visit some of the men's taverns and see if I hear anything."

Maria got up and began pacing back and forth; if she didn't look so serious, he would have thought it was cute. "The Ablaians are only part of the problem. The men joined them out of their own free will because of the way we treat them. Even if we stop every Ablaian plot, sooner or later, we will still have problems if we don't fix how we treat the men."

Thad had thought the same thing but was unsure of how to broach the topic with the princess; he had few people he could talk to and didn't want to alienate any-one from his small circle of friends.

Bruno kept his end of the bargain and delivered the swords a few days ahead of schedule. Considering the timeline he had been given, he produced four swords a day, allowing him to work on projects from his bac-klist of orders as well as his sending box. Maria would stop by every few days to talk and inspect what he was working on. He found that when he was stumped by a difficult project, bouncing ideas off her helped. More than once, she came up with a solution that he would have never thought of. He had been having an incredibly difficult time finding out how to make the sending boxes when the princess asked him if he could just make the insides like a hallway. While the idea struck him as funny, the more he thought about it, the more it made sense. He had learned magic didn't exist in a normal fashion but lived on a subdimension, waiting to be pul-led on by a mage. If he could build a magical room in a subdimension where the box lids were the doors to the room but only one could be opened at a time, it could work. The only problem was what would happen if the box was ever destroyed; he would have to put in sube-nchantments to cause the room to collapse on itself, and just to be safe, the boxes would have to be made solidly out of metal and not wood. And if he wanted to make one box able to communicate with several, maybe he could make a revolving room. It seemed possible, but just testing the idea on a small scale would require more gold and time than he currently had to waste, so he put the idea to the side and continued with enchanting the swords.

He finished the swords a few weeks ahead of schedule and, over a two-day period, moved them back to his house and replaced them in the wooden crates Bruno had sent them over in. With them crated, he only needed a way to get them to the palace, so he went out and purchased a one-horse wagon.

He was quickly let into the palace grounds, and a host of slaves unloaded his wares and transported them to the guards' training ground. After a couple hours' wait, he was soon graced with the presence of the queen and princess, who greeted him fondly. "What have you brought us?"

He signaled for one of the slaves to open up the nearest crate. He picked up the first sword and walked over to one of the training pells and with one deft stroke cut the man-sized pell in half, securing gasps of asto-nishment from his viewers. "From what I was told, each sword is magically strengthened to withstand massive blows, as well as magically sharpened to cut through your opponents."

The queen nodded to one of her guards, who picked up one of the swords and took it through a series of strikes, then attacked the pells, cutting a score of them into firewood. He gave the sword an appraising look and replaced it back in the crate. "They are well balanced and cut through the pells with little resistance. I would be honored to have such a blade at my disposal, Your Majesty."

"As per our agreement, I will have the 1,500 gold sent to the local money changers in your name. I would also like to order two hundred more swords and three hundred shields to be used by my personal guard."

"Your Majesty, I can't give you an exact time frame for my source to be able to prepare such an order, but I will do my best to see that it is done," Thad said, trying to hide his irritation.

The queen smiled slightly. "Tell your source there is no rush and that he may send them as he has time. I will pay the aforementioned fifteen gold per sword and ten gold per shield. The price is non-negotiable. Now if you would excuse me, I have prior engagements I must attend to."

CHAPTER IX

With the sale of the swords, Thad had more gold than he could honestly spend even after paying off the loan for the house. The money changers had given him a small booklet of fine paper to use for notes of payment, for large payments as well as recording the signet ring that he had gotten from Monique to verify payments.

With a new energy in his step, Thad made his way to the blacksmith, where he was greeted by a happy Margret. "Have you come to make another large order, Lady Clair?"

"Yes, I have. Is Bruno available? While I will need more swords, there are a few other things I would like him to make that need to be made to a specific design."

"For one of our distinguished customers, I am sure he will be more than willing to step away from whatever he is doing," she said before disappearing to the back of the smithy.

Bruno came out with his normal bluster about being bothered while he worked. Thad was sure it was done more to annoy Margret than for any practical reason. "Master smith, just the person I needed to see. I have a couple of new projects, and I find myself in the need of your assistance again." Bruno gave him a look that was in between a smile and a smirk as he launched into the details of what he needed.

"Well, Lady Clair, the swords can be made easily enough now that the molds are already made. The shields will take a bit of time to make a mold for, though I don't know why you want the metal so thin, but that's your decision. The chests you're asking for are the real problem. Making something fit as tight as that will take a bit of working, and the five large ones even more work, and lining the inside with silver won't be easy or cheap. I'm sure I can get it all done, but it's going to take some time. I hope you're not in too much of a hurry."

"No, I'm not in too much of a hurry, Master Bruno, but as you get the items made, I would like them delivered. The main question here to me is the cost."

Bruno and Margret stepped aside and talked among themselves, Margret jotting down notes on a sheet of paper every now and then. When they were done talking, Margret turned back to him, her smile as big as ever. "For everything—swords, shields, and chests—it will be a total of 1,200 gold."

Thad had to keep from fainting upon hearing the cost, but thinking about it, he should have expected it. He had been doing well with all his projects. He had slightly over two hundred gold hidden at his home, but even that and what he had left at the money changers were barely enough to cover the expense.

After a long bout of haggling, he was able to get Margret to come down to 1,080 gold, with half paid up front and the rest paid in increments as the products were delivered.

With nothing else pressing to work on until Bruno delivered some of his orders, he began working on the many orders requested by the nobles. Most of the requests were simple and boring things that didn't attract his interest, but from time to time, they would ask for something that presented him with a challenge.

The days passed by fairly quickly with him working in the sewer during the day and prowling the seedier taverns at night. Most of the time, he got the same feeling from the patrons of the taverns; they were unhappy, but there were no diabolic plots.

Shariel was proceeding well with her studies and seemed to enjoy herself at the school. She had a natural charisma and seemed to make many friends, many of whom she brought over quite often. He was glad she was adjusting so well to her new life, but the constant need to hold his disguise while at home was getting annoying.

The swords came, along with two of the smaller chests he had ordered. The chests were sized to fit a few small letters; while not very big, they were perfect for trying out his idea before wasting time and money on the bigger ones. He had to get the sending chest ench-antment perfect before trying it on the larger ones since they would have to be done at the house, being too large to fit in any of the sewer entrances.

With the two small chests in his sack, he quickly made his way to the sewer to begin his work. With all the metal work already done for him, all he had to do was place the gem and start enchanting. Not having to tax his strength to manipulate the metal himself was refreshing. He was a little wary of starting the project without alerting the princess since doing something new, especially something as complicated as this, required complete concentration, until he completely understood where he could stop without the enchantment collapsing.

While he didn't want to start on the project without someone to watch out for him, the urge to do so was almost unbearable. When he was about to give in to his desire, the princess was nice enough to grace him with her presence. "I could almost kiss you. I was hoping you would visit today."

The princess's face burned bright red, then she closed her eyes. "Well, if you must." she replied. Everything clicked in place for him as he watched her stand there, blushing with her eyes closed tight. She was only a few years younger than him, and when she got older, she promised to be a sight to behold, and he had to admit she intrigued him. So with a slight chuckle, he leaned in and gave her a light kiss on the cheek, his own face burning bright red.

He then hurried to explain what he was going to try to do as well as the dangers involved. The princess didn't like the idea but finally agreed to make sure he got water and broth at least once a day and that if it looked like it was too much for him to find a way to force a break in his concentration, but it cost him a second kiss.

It took two days for him to finish the sending boxes; it would have been quicker, but it took a while to figure out how to link the extra dimensional room attached to the boxes, though once that was done, it was simple enough to attach the rooms so that no matter where they were, they were essentially the same box on the inside. To test the new sending boxes, he gave one to the princess while taking the other back to his house, where he put in a simple note asking if it worked. After reading a bit from his magical tome, he opened the sending box to find a note written in flowing script simply saying yes. It had worked; whether it would work at long distances was unknown, but Thad could think of no reason that it wouldn't.

Each morning and night, he would check his sending box to see if anything was in there. He really needed a way for it to let him know as soon as anything was present inside the box, but that could be done on his next set. He still had to try allowing one box to reach multiple ones.

As his orders arrived from Bruno, he went to work to finish them as quickly as possible so he could keep enough gold available to keep all the bills paid. By the time the first large chest had arrived, Thad had already completed over two-thirds of the swords and around a hundred of the shields. Bruno had let him know that once the molds were finished on the shields, he would focus all his attention on the chests, but even so, it would take a long time to complete them. With Bruno paid and the amount of gold in his account steadily growing with each delivery to the palace, Thad began to slow down his work. Shariel and Maria had been harassing him about his health because days of working with little breaks and skipped meals were starting to show. The muscle definition of his body from years of sword practice and exercise had faded, and he had lost a considerable amount of weight.

Limiting himself to only four hours a day to work and the rest to regaining his strength seemed daunting at first, but as his health returned, so did his stamina. He hadn't realized it, but he had felt tired and more lethargic lately. He gave himself a mental kick, wondering why he had let himself get to such a state. Magic and gold were all well and good, but if it cost him his health, there was no point to it. After two weeks of his new routine, he felt great and had a much livelier bounce in his steep.

While he worked on projects for the queen, many other orders were coming in at an alarming rate, but he tried to push that thought aside; he had never promised anyone that what they wanted would or could be done, but he still made sure to look over each request to see if anything struck his mind. One of the ideas finally did; it was a grand idea and one that would be of great use. A baroness had wanted to know if he could get her a mag-ical item that would allow her to cook without fire. He had already found out that any spell using fire would cause the item focusing it to absorb heat. If he were to have a large stone with the top layered with steel, he should be able to make a fireless cooking device.

Shariel had school, and the princess would be occupied all day with affairs of state, so he didn't think they would notice if he skipped his early-morning pra-ctice and went to work a little earlier than normal. As he made his way to his usual sewer entrance in the squ-atters' district, he heard voices from his normal alle-yway. The sun had barely peeked about the horizon; most people were either asleep or on their way to attend to their business, not hanging around in a dead-end alley.

"Listen, it's perfect. We already have some of the queen's guards and enough of the servants to allow us in the palace. All we have to do is strike and kill her and that little bitch of a child. With them dead, it will be that much easier to get what we want," the man said loudly but was quickly hushed by the others he was with. Thad couldn't make out much of the rest of the conversation other than it was to happen soon at a party.

Not wanting to be noticed, Thad silently went back the way he had come and headed straight for his house and the sending box to warn the princess. Reaching his house, he quickly dashed up the stairs and hastily scribbled "You are in danger, not safe with guards, attack soon at a party, stay safe" on a piece of paper.

Thad nervously checked the sending box every few minutes to see if Maria had gotten his note yet. When he opened it and the note was gone, he relaxed a little but kept checking in case she left a reply. After what seemed like a lifetime, a response finally appeared. "Party in three days, I will make sure you are invited."

Three days wasn't much time, and the only way into the palace was to enter disguised as Clair. He wouldn't be able to take any large weapons, so his sword and staff were out of the question. He would have to think of something else. He would also have to make sure that if anything happened to him, Shariel would still be taken care of, so he made a quick stop at the money-lenders' guild.

After everything he had sold to the palace and his other special orders, the account held slightly over three thousand gold. So far, only his name and Monique's were allowed to access the account. Thinking it not a good idea to let Shariel have control over all the money, he had one thousand gold deposited into a separate account and paid a small fee to have a signet ring made for Shariel. Now if anything happened to him, she should have more than enough money to see her through school and help her with whatever future she decided.

While he waited for Shariel to get home, he went through a list of ideas to help him in case trouble hit at the palace. He needed a sword, but he would never be allowed to take one inside the palace. The closest he could get swords to was the palace grounds, and that was if they were crated. If he could just make a sword that would appear at his command, that would be nice, but he had no idea how that would work. But what if he made a sword that would form on his command? He had already formed metal with magic hundreds of times; if he were to make a enchantment to merely form metal into the shape of a sword, then all he would have to carry would be the raw materials, but how? Then it hit him. What if he got a dagger with a thick blade? He could enchant it to lengthen the metal. The end result would be thin, but if he worked it right, it would be just as strong, if not as strong, as the ones he had made for the queen's guard. As for his staff, there was no need to make a miniature one seeing as he already had one. It wasn't as powerful, but it was the best he could do in such a short amount of time.

After a quick search through the different weapons shops in town, he finally found a dagger that would work perfectly. It had a large handle made of wood with a metal cross guard. The blade was longer than normal, being almost a foot long with a thick base narrowing down and curving slightly toward the point. It was a little awkward strapped to his leg, but for his purpose, it would work perfectly. He also stopped by the jewelry store and purchased two large diamonds for the dagger. Cat's-eye gems were good, but the sheer amount of magic he would need to shape the metal in a moment's notice was more than the cheap gems could handle.

He didn't want to risk going back to his lair, so he began working on the dagger at his home. He had both diamonds set in place before Shariel got home. She was in a good mood when she came in, carrying one of the magical tomes he had made for her. She had filled it with some educational books, but most of them were simply for fancy. He had made the tome especially for her. She had first used the original, but she complained that once a book was copied, it couldn't be removed; he thought the idea was a good one, so made her one where she could exchange the books at will.

"Shariel, we need to talk." His voice was serious, leaving little doubt that what he was going to tell her was important. Her demeanor suddenly changed from carefree to worried since the last time he had talked to her in such a way was before he went off to fight the bandits. He could understand her concern. He explained what he had learned and that he was going to be present to help protect the queen and princess. "The queen really doesn't like me, so even if everything goes right, I might have to leave for some time."

She didn't understand why the queen would want to do anything bad to him if he helped. "If you help her, shouldn't she give you a reward?"

Sometimes he forgot how innocent she was. She had been through so much already, and he didn't want to pile any more hardship on her small shoulders, but he couldn't let the queen and princess die when he had a chance to stop it. Overall, Shariel seemed to take it a lot better than he had foreseen, but late that night, he could hear her crying from his room. Each sob seemed to tear a little more into his soul.

CHAPTER X

Thad strapped his gear on, hoping it would be enough. His new dagger sword, his miniature staff, his rune necklace, his various rings, and a new shield plate that looked like a silver disk with small cat's-eye gems circling a larger one. It would allow protection for a large area. It only worked within a ten-square-foot box, but it would hopefully be enough to protect the queen and princess for around half an hour.

The palace gates were swarming with people waiting to get into the party. Many of them he knew from their orders, and everyone that saw him made polite conversation, casually bringing up how much they liked or couldn't wait to get what they had requested. It was maddening having to listen to them rattle on about each magical creation, trying to outdo the others in every facet of their lives, from how many slaves they owned to how much money they had spent on a prized horse. Thad could have almost screamed with relief when he finally made his way past the gates into the palace proper.

It didn't take long for him to locate the princess, who was surrounded by a group of giggling girls of all ages. She was wearing a light blue dress that seemed to float around her. She was smiling, but he could see a strained quality to it; noticing him, the tension almost visibly drained away. Maria waved him over; he could see her bouncing slightly on her feet as he made his way to her. Even though the reason for his visit was a serious one, the sight still brought a smile to his face.

Maria gave him a quick hug and then introduced him to everyone, which, of course, resulted in an instant bombardment of questions about the magical items he had been procuring for their parents. He was starting to feel overwhelmed; everyone knew who he was, and many of them knew Shariel as well, but he was having a hard time connecting the names with all the faces. Luckily, the princess saved him by switching the conversations away from him and over to royal gossip.

The first few hours of the party were simply to allow the guests to comingle and talk. Not Thad's favorite pastime, but it did allow him to freely move around and look for anything out of the ordinary. He did learn that each member of the patronage who did not own local buildings had brought along a host of retainers who were staying with them in the palace for the night, most of whom were supposed to be preparing their ladies' rooms for when they retired. Even those that did have housing within the city had brought along a half-dozen servants to take care of the coaches they had arrived in as well as personal guard for the short trip to and from their residences. Every slave and servant was under suspicion in his mind, and there was a great number of them.

As soon as the opportunity occurred, he pulled the princess aside and asked her how the night would proceed. She was a little pouty at first since he had not commented on her dress or the way she had done her hair, and after an apology, she smiled and started explaining the course of the night's events.

"First, we mingle, allowing anyone who has pressing matters with one lady or another to prepare for the eventuality of a meeting. This will be the time that they use to set up such meetings, then we shall have a formal dinner, where we will be seated by rank and privileges. Sadly, you will not be allowed to sit next to me, but hopefully, Mother won't have you seated too far down. Finally, we will have music and more mingling, where my mother will pull different individuals into private meetings for one reason or another. The meeting room is in a small room at the rear of the ballroom. There is only one way in or out. No secret passage and the only guard allowed inside is Mother's guard captain."

Thad ran his fingers through his hair. If the captain was involved, the infiltrators would wait to attack until the queen was in the room. If not, they would attack during the meal. It would allow for the most confusion as well as allow them to conceal the most hostiles within the room. "I need to be as close the queen as possible during the meal, Maria."

Maria looked at him for a few moments as if her eyes were searching for something. "I'll ask her to have you seated next to me. It might offend a few people, but we can always play it off as trying to get reduced cost on magical items. Believe it or not, most of the room is abuzz with rumors about you." Maria flashed him a wry grin, knowing that he hated all the attention.

Maria introduced him to many of the more prom-inent nobles, each of them fascinated by the magical weapons he had procured for the queen. Most of them visibly cringed at the cost of outfitting their own armies and tried to get him to commit to a lower per-item cost for a bulk order. He put each of them off, saying that he would have to consult with his supplier and get in touch with them at a future point in time. They all took it well, many of them smiling as if he had already agreed. In most cases, a foreign merchant, which he was pretending to be, would be at their mercy, but he was the only known supplier of magical items, so he didn't fear they would cause him too much trouble in the future.

Maria finally led him to where the queen sat on an ornament chair. Just like with his previous visit, there was a long line of people who offered their greetings and gifts. Maria had forewarned him, so Thad had prepared a gift suitable for the queen; it was a silver disk that filled the room with illusionary butterflies. He had gotten the idea from one of his orders that had wanted illusionary flowers to fill her dining room for one of her parties.

It didn't take too long for him and the princess to reach the front of the line. The queen gave him an app-roving smile as he approached and gave her a deep bow, holding his gift out in front of him. "Your Majesty, I humbly present you with this small token of my app-reciation for allowing me to grace your party. Touch the center gem, and your room will be filled with a display nearly as beautiful as your own presence."

The queen wasted no time in turning on the device, and hundreds of butterflies filled the room, fluttering around. There were plenty of gasps of astonishment, and he noticed more than a few people reaching out toward the fake butterflies. He smiled as their faces turned to surprise as they landed on their fingers. He had worked hard to make them as real as possible, even to the touch. "You have outdone yourself again, Lady Clair. It is a most wonderful gift. I shall have to invite you to more of my gatherings if you continue to shower me with such opulent gifts."

As soon as he was out of line, he was quickly and quietly pulled aside by the princess. "That was marvelous. I don't think I will have any trouble getting you a seat next to me, but I expect that you will be getting a torrent of invites for every party thrown in the queendom." The princess giggled as she looked around the room. Thad followed her and noticed that all the eyes in the room were on him, and he could hear his name said more than once, though with the noise in the room, he couldn't tell exactly what was being said.

Maria wasn't too far off the mark. As soon as the commotion died down, he was assaulted by offers to come visit various estates all over Farlan and even by foreign dignitaries who invited him to their kingdom, promising him the best accommodations and entertainment. Maria seemed to be enjoying his distress as he tried to deftly dodge their invitations without offending anyone. When Maria disappeared from his side to attend to other matters, the invitations got more insistent and extravagant. When it was announced that the dinner would soon be served, he could have jumped for joy.

Everyone was guided from the room and led to their seat by a personal servant. The queen and Maria were sat at the head of the table, and he let out a sigh of relief when he was sat at Maria's left side. As the first course was brought out, a small salad with fresh cheese and tomatoes delicately carved to look like flowers, he watched the servers for any sign of weapons. Each wore plain dark-colored clothing that hung loosely on their bodies, but he could detect no hint of any weapons being hidden within. He started to think that his fears were unfounded when the main course was brought in, a small fowl covered in a rich white sauce garnished with some sort of nut. As he took his second bite of the juicy white meat, trying to discern what the sauce could have been made from, a scream echoed through the hall.

Thad never got to see who had screamed as his vision was locked on the mass of slaves that were piling in from the server's entrance loaded with three or four swords each. Many of the servants rushed to their comrades, taking a weapon and spreading out, while others ran from the room. The two guards, one on each side of the queen, drew their swords and took a defe-nsive stance. One of the guards Thad recognized as the queen's guard captain, who had soundly beat him back at the academy.

A few moments later, the whole room was filled with queen's guard, and Thad was beginning to think his assistance wouldn't be needed but decided to stay near the princess in any case. Then the situation took a turn for the worse as the guards at the back struck out at their fellow guards, felling over half of them with their initial strike. As the guards fought against themselves, the host of armed servants made their way toward where the queen and princess sat. The queen's personal guards were outnumbered twenty to one, so, sighing, Thad pulled the sword from a hidden slit in his dress and, with a flick of his wrist, brought it to its full length.

The guard nearest him quickly noticed his action and pulled the princess defensively behind him. Thad just gave the man a wry smile and moved on the servants who were cautiously advancing toward them. Thad quickly went through his options. He couldn't use his area-paralyzing spell; it would stop everyone, and he honestly didn't know who the good ones and the bad ones were. Most of his offensive spells would have to be limited to individuals in order to not accidentally hit one of the guests. He had given his protective disk to the princess earlier and only hoped she remembered to use it.

Thad closed the last few feet, quickly attacking, his sword whistling as it cut through the air. The first two attackers went down quick as his sword cut through their blades and bodies as if they were made of parc-hment, but then he had to duck and dodge as blows came from every direction. He thought about turning on his shield, but it would cover everything, including his sword, making him useless in a close fight. Two more fell to his blade before one of the men got a strike thro-ugh his guard, cutting a deep slash across his face and sending a torrent of pain through his body. He could hear the princess scream as he rolled back, away from his attackers.

Blood flowed freely from his wound into his eye, effectively blinding him in his right eye. Two of the men broke off from the group as the rest continued on to where the queen and princess waited. As he got to his feet, he could see the attackers' and the two defending guards' swords stop inches in the air from each other to the surprise of both parties. Thad's smile disappeared quickly as the men turned their attention back on him.

His options disappearing fast, Thad reached for his miniature staff as he parried an overhead strike from one man while sidestepping a strike aimed for his mids-ection by another. With his staff free and the queen and Maria safely behind the shield, he let loose a torrent of powerful lighting strikes, felling over two dozen in the first wave. The few remaining backed away slowly, watching and waiting for him to make his next move. He spared a glance over to where the guards were finishing off whoever the losers were. His nerves tightened as the fighting ended, and the remaining guards advanced on where he and the attackers were at a stalemate. He didn't know which side they were on, but in the off chance they were the good guys, he couldn't let loose another array of bolts without jeopardizing them as well, and he didn't want to do that if they were friendly.

The attackers must not have known for sure whose side they were on either as they attacked him with renewed vigor. He parried attack after attack, trying to find a rhythm, attacking back whenever an opening appeared, though with the number of people attacking him, there were few. In the few seconds it took the guards to reach him, he had already sustained a score of wounds, but to his relief, the guards quickly struck down the remaining attackers in short order.

Thad, breathing hard and bleeding profusely from his many wounds, sat down heavily on the ground. He noticed the princess was being taken from the room by the guard who had pulled her to safety earlier. Looking around for the queen, he noticed that she was slowly walking toward him. There was a large smile on her face. He didn't know what she was so happy about but hoped it didn't bode ill for him. He had brought a sword into the queen's presence, but he had only used it to protect her.

The queen squatted down, her hand softly cupping his face to bring his eyes up to look at her. "My dear, dear Mark, I had assumed you were the supplier to the Rose Company, though I will admit, I never susp-ected that you were Clair. Such a clever disguise. We will have to have a long discussion on what to do about your punishment."

Thad panicked. He had been so absorbed in the fight he had dropped his disguise. As he tried to clear his mind enough to make an escape, one of the guards blew a white powder in his face, and he had to fight to keep his eyes open. He could feel himself being picked up from the ground by strong hands. He tried to resist and shake free of their grip, but his body would not heed his commands.

EPILOGUE

Thad hurt all over as he regained consciousness. Everything around him was dark, and he was lying on a hard surface. He tried to sit up, but he found his legs and arms were chained to his bed. He could feel a light buzzing in the back of his mind as he tried to clear his thoughts. Focusing on his chains, he tried to make the metal flow away from his body, but nothing happened. Thinking to try something easier, he focused on a light. A dim flicker appeared in his hand for a mere moment before flickering out. He was a prisoner, and he couldn't perform even the most simple of spells. He was doomed.

After what seemed like hours, but might have only been moments, he could hear footsteps coming toward him. After a few moments, a bright light assaulted his eyes, and he could hear talking, but in his muddled state of mind, it was hard to make out the words. As his eyes adjusted to the light, he noticed the queen as well as two of her guards had come to visit him.

"I see you're finally awake. We had begun to worry that we hadn't gotten the mixture right when you hadn't woken up after two days. You see, while know-ledge of magic has disappeared from the history books, the knowledge of how to deal with mages has not." The queen let out a long sigh as she ran her fingers down his bare chest. "My daughter is quite upset with me, but one day, she will understand. We can't just have a rogue mage doing what he pleases within our realm. If you vow to honor my ownership and act accordingly, I will set you free, but be warned if you run—I will spare no expense in hunting you and that little girl of yours down. What was her name,

Shariel? We already have men shadowing her just in case. If you were to escape, they have orders to kill her. Do we have an understanding?"

Thad tried to sit up but was defeated by his bonds. "I will never be a slave. You may kill me, but if you touch one hair on Shariel's head, I will kill you." Thad tried for menacing, but it came out in more of a crackling whisper.

The queen gave a slight chuckle as she drove her finger hard into his chest. "We will see if you sing a different tune after a few weeks of our hospitality."

Made in the USA
San Bernardino, CA
11 April 2014